INTERNATIONAL POCKET LIBRARY

EDITED BY EDMUND R. BROWN

*[handwritten annotations:]*
★ Jacob Riis ➔ 1880s-90s
Pictures of US slums in cities,
Used to gain awareness of upper class
4/17/04 ★

# THE LOWER DEPTHS

*[handwritten annotations:]*
- environment shapes character
- different dialects, but all "speak
in one voice."

★ Will they climb out of the
lower depths? ➔ group
Plot question

# THE LOWER DEPTHS

## (*Nachtasyl*)

### Scenes from Russian Life
### BY MAXIM GORKI

*Translated from the Russian by Edwin Hopkins*

BOSTON

INTERNATIONAL POCKET LIBRARY

**BRANDEN PUBLISHING COMPANY**
17 Station Street
Box 843 Brookline Village
Boston,  MA 02147

# DRAMATIS PERSONAE

(In the order in which they first speak in the play)

A BARON, *32 years old.*

KVASCHNYA, *a huckstress, towards* 40.

BUBNOFF, *a capmaker,* 45.

KLESHTSCH, ANDREW MITRITCH, *locksmith,* 40.

NASTIAH, 24.

ANNA, *wife of* KLESHTSCH, 30.

SAHTIN, 40.

AN ACTOR, 40.

KOSTILIOFF, MICHAEL IVANOWITCH, *lodging-house keeper,* 54.

PEPEL, WASKA, 28.

NATASHA, *sister of* WASSILISSA, 20.

LUKA, *a pilgrim,* 60.

ALYOSHKA, *a shoemaker,* 20.

WASSILISSA KARPOVNA, *wife of* KOSTILIOFF, 26.

MEDVIÉDEFF, *uncle of* WASSILISSA, *policeman,* 50.

A TARTAR, 40, *a porter.*

KRIVOI ZOBA, 40, *a porter.*

   *Several nameless tramps, supernumeraries.*

# ACT I

*A basement-room resembling a cavern. The massive, vaulted stone ceiling is blackened with smoke, its rough plaster in places broken off. The light falls inwardly from above, through a square window on the left (of one facing the footlights). The left corner,* PEPEL'S *quarter, is separated from the rest of the room by thin partitions, against which, extending from beneath the window towards C. is* BUBNOFF'S *bunk.*

*In the right corner is a great Russian stove, the rear of which is set into the wall which arches over it, the portion of the stove which extends into the room being an incline up which the personages must scramble to reach the space under the archway.*

*In the massive wall to the right is a door to the kitchen, in which* KVASCHNYA, *the* BARON, *and* NASTIAH *live.*

*Below the window, on the left, is a broad bed with dirty cotton curtains. Slightly L. C. (adjoining* PEPEL'S *room) a flight of a few steps leads back to a platform, from which, to the left and behind* PEPEL'S *room, lead other steps, to an entry or hallway.*

*A door opens inwardly on this platform, while to the right another flight of stairs leads to a room R. U. E. over the stove, in which the proprietor and his family live. The*

7

*balustrade is in a bad condition and a torn rug or quilt lies over it.*

*Between the stove and the short flight of steps a pritsche (a sort of broad low bench with four legs, which serves as a bunk). Another such bunk is across the front of the stove, and a third is at the right below the door to the kitchen. Near this is a wooden block to which is secured a small anvil and vise.* KLESHTSCH *sits on a smaller block, at work on a pair of old locks, into which he is fitting keys. At his feet are two bundles of keys of various sizes, strung on wire hoops, and a damaged samovar (a sort of tea urn commonly used in Russia), a hammer and some files.*

*In the middle of the room a great table, two benches, and a heavy tabouret, all unpainted and dirty.* KVASCHNYA, *at the table R. cleaning a samovar, acts as housekeeper, while the* BARON *L. C. chews on a piece of black bread, and* NASTIAH *L. sits on the tabouret, her elbows on the table, her face in her hands, reading a tattered book.* ANNA, *in bed, concealed by the curtains is frequently heard coughing.* BUBNOFF *sits, tailor fashion on his bench, measuring off on a form which he holds between his knees, the pieces of an old pair of trousers which he has ripped up, cutting out caps to the best advantage. Behind him is a smashed hatbox from which he cuts visors, stacking the perfect ones on two nails in the partition and throwing the useless ones about the room. Around him are bits of oilcloth and scraps.*

SAHTIN, *just awakening, on the pritsche before the stove, grumbles and roars. On the stove, hidden by the left springer of the arch, the* ACTOR *is heard coughing and turning.*

Time: *Early Spring. Morning.*

BARON. Go on. (*Desiring more of the story.*)

KVASCHNYA. Never, I tell you, my friend—take it away. I've been through it all, I want you to know. No treasure could tempt me to marry again. (SAHTIN *grunts at this.*)

BUBNOFF (*to* SAHTIN). What are you grunting about?

KVASCHNYA. I, a free woman, my own boss, shall I register my name in somebody else's passport, become a man's serf, when nobody can say 'that' to me now? Don't let me dream about it. I'll never do it. If he were a prince out of America—I wouldn't have him!

KLESHTSCH. You lie.

KVASCHNYA (*turning toward him*). Wh-at! (*Turns back.*)

KLESHTSCH. You are lying. You are going to marry Abram.

BARON (*rises, takes* NASTIAH's *book and reads the title*). 'Disastrous Love.' (*Laughs.*)

NASTIAH (*reaches for the book*). Here! Give it back. Now; stop your joke.

(*The* BARON *eyes her and waves the book in the air.*)

KVASCHNYA (*to* KLESHTSCH *again*). You lie, you red-headed billy goat; speaking to me like that, the nerve of it!

BARON (*gives* NASTIAH *a blow on the head with the book*). What a stupid goose you are, Nastiah.

NASTIAH. Give it here (*snatches the book*).

KLESHTSCH (*to* KVASCHNYA). You are a great lady! . . . But just the same you'll be Abram's wife . . . That is what you want.

KVASCHNYA. Certainly (*spoken ironically*). To be sure . . . What else . . . And you beating your wife half to death.

KLESHTSCH (*furiously*).  Hold your snout, old slut! What's that to you?

KVASCHNYA (*shouting*).  Ah, ha! You can't listen to the truth!

BARON.  Now, they're let loose. Nastiah,—where are you?

NASTIAH (*without raising her head*).  What? let me alone!

ANNA (*putting her head out of the bed curtains*).  It is dawning already. For Heaven's sake! Stop screaming and quarrelling.

KLESHTSCH.  Croaking again! (*Contemptuously.*)

ANNA.  Every day that God gives, you quarrel. Let me at least die in quiet.

BUBNOFF.  The noise don't keep you from dying.

KVASCHNYA (*goes to* ANNA).  Tell me, Anna dear, how have you endured such a brute?

ANNA.  Let me be! Let me—

KVSACHNYA.  Now, now, you poor martyr. Still no better with your breast?

BARON.  It is time for us to go to market, Kvaschnya.

KVASCHNYA.  Then let's go now. (*To* ANNA) Would you like a cup of hot custard?

ANNA.  I don't need it; thank you, though. Why should I still eat?

KVASCHNYA.  Oh, eat! Hot food is always good. It is quieting. I will put it away for you in a cup and when your appetite comes, then eat. (*To the* BARON) Let's go, sir. (*To* KLESHTSCH, *going around him*)  Huh! you Satan!

ANNA (*coughing*).  Oh, God!

BARON (*jostles* NASTIAH *on the nape of the neck*). Drop it . . . you goose.

NASTIAH (*murmurs*). Go on. I am not in your way. (*Turns a page. The* BARON *whistles in derision; crosses to R. Ex. into kitchen following* KVASCHNYA.)

SAHTIN (*gets up from his pritsche*). Who was it that beat me up yesterday?

BUBNOFF. That's all the same to you.

SAHTIN. Suppose it is. But what for?

BUBNOFF. You played cards?

SAHTIN. Played cards? Oh, so I did.

BUBNOFF. That's why.

SAHTIN. Crooks!

ACTOR (*on the stove, thrusting his head out*). They'll kill you once, some day.

SAHTIN. You are—a blockhead!

ACTOR. Why so?

SAHTIN. They could not kill me twice.

ACTOR (*after a short silence*). I don't see it.—Why not?

KLESHTSCH (*turning to him*). Crawl down off the stove and clean the place up! You're too finiky, anyhow.

ACTOR. That's none of your business . . .

KLESHTSCH. Wait! . . . When Wassilissa comes she will show you whose business it is.

ACTOR. The devil take Wassilissa. The Baron must straighten up today, it's his turn . . . Baron!

BARON (*enters R. from kitchen*). I haven't time. I must go to market with Kvaschnya.

ACTOR. That's nothing to me . . . Go to Siberia for my sake . . . but the floor must be swept up and it's your turn . . . Don't imagine that I will do somebody else's work.

BARON (*crosses to* NASTIAH). No? Then the devil take

you! Nastengka will sweep up a little. Say! You! 'Disastrous Love!' Wake up! (*Takes the book.*)

NASTIAH (*rising*). What do you want? Give it here, mischief maker. And this is a nobleman!

BARON (*gives the book back*). Nastiah! Do a little bit of sweeping for me—will you?

NASTIAH (*goes R. Ex. R. into kitchen*). Sure, I'm crazy to.

KVASCHNYA (*within, to the* BARON). Come along. They can certainly clean up without you. (*Ex.* BARON *R.*) You, Actor, you must do it. You were asked to do it, so do it then. It won't break your back.

ACTOR. Now, always I—h'm—I can't understand it. (*The* BARON *enters from the kitchen carrying, by means of a yoke, two baskets in which are fat jars covered with rags.*)

BARON. Pretty heavy to-day.

SAHTIN. You could do that without being a baron.

KVASCHNYA (*to the* ACTOR). See to it that you sweep up. (*Ex. to the entry L. U. E. preceded by the* BARON.)

ACTOR (*crawls down from the stove*). I must not inhale dust. It injures me (*self-pityingly*). My organism is poisoned with alcohol. (*Sits introspectively on the pritsche before the stove.*)

SAHTIN. Orgism. Organism (*derisively*).

ANNA (*to* KLESHTSCH). Ahndrey Mitrisch—

KLESHTSCH. What is the matter now?

ANNA. Kvaschnya left some custard for me. Go, eat it.

KLESHTSCH (*crosses to her*). Won't you eat?

ANNA. I won't. Why should I eat? You—work. You must eat.

KLESHTSCH. Are you afraid? Do not despair. Perhaps you'll be better again.

ANNA. Go, eat. My heart is grieved; the end is near.

KLESHTSCH (*moves away*). Oh, no; perhaps—you can get up yet—such things have happened. (*Ex. R. into kitchen.*)

ACTOR (*loudly, as though suddenly awakened from a dream*). Yesterday, in the dispensary, the doctor said to me: 'Your organism is poisoned with alcohol, through and through.'

SAHTIN (*laughing*). Orgism!

ACTOR (*with emphasis*). Not orgism, but organism—or-gan-is-m.

SAHTIN. Sigambrer!

ACTOR (*with a deprecating movement of the hand*). Ah! gibberish. I speak in earnest, indeed. My organism is poisoned . . . so that I shall be injured if I sweep the room . . . and breathe the dust.

SAHTIN. Microbites . . . ha!

BUBNOFF. What are you muttering about?

SAHTIN. Words . . . then there is still another word: transcendental.

BUBNOFF. What does that mean?

SAHTIN. I don't know, I've forgotten.

BUBNOFF. Why do you say it then?

SAHTIN. Just so . . . I'm tired of all our words, Bubnoff. Every one of them I've heard at least a thousand times.

ACTOR. As it says in Hamlet, 'Words, words, words,' A magnificent piece, 'Hamlet'—I've played the grave digger.

KLESHTSCH (*entering R. from the kitchen*). Will you begin to play the broom?

ACTOR. That's very little to you (*strikes his breast with his fist*). 'The fair Ophelia! Nymph in thy orison, Be all my sins remembered!' (*Within, somewhere in the distance, a dull sound is heard, cries, and the shrill sound of a policeman's whistle.* KLESHTSH *sits down to work and the rasping of his file is heard.*)

SAHTIN. I love the incromprehensible rare words. As a young man I was in the telegraph service. I have read many books.

BUBNOFF. So you have been a telegraph operator?

SAHTIN. To be sure (*laughs*). Many beautiful books exist, and a lot of curious words. I was a man of education, understand that?

BUBNOFF. I've already heard so, a hundred times. What does the world care what a man was. I, for example, was a furrier, had my own place of business. My arm was quite yellow—from the dye, when I colored the furs—quite yellow, my friend, up to the elbow. I thought that my whole life long I could never wash it clean, would descend, with yellow hands, into my grave, and now look at them, they are—simply dirty, see!

SAHTIN. And what more?

BUBNOFF. Nothing more.

SAHTIN. What of it all?

BUBNOFF. I mean only . . . by way of example . . . no matter how gaily a man lays the color on, it all rubs off again . . . all off again! See!

SAHTIN. Hm! . . . My bones ache!

ACTOR (*sits on the pritsche before the stove, his arms*

*over his knees).* Education is a rigmarole, the main thing is genius. I once knew an actor . . . he could scarcely read the words of his part, but he played his hero so that the walls of the theatre shook with the ecstasy of the public . . .

SAHTIN. Bubnoff, give me five copecs.

BUBNOFF. I've only two myself.

ACTOR. I say, genius a leading man must have. Genius —believe in yourself, in your own power . . .

SAHTIN. Give me a fiver and I will believe that you are a genius, a hero, a crocodile, a precinct captain. Kleshtsch, give me a fiver.

KLESHTSCH. Go to the devil. There are too many ragamuffins about.

SAHTIN. Stop scolding; I know you have nothing.

ANNA. Andrew Mitrisch . . . It is suffocating. It is hard . . .

KLESHTSCH. What can I do about that?

BUBNOFF. Open the door to the street floor.

KLESHTSCH. Well said! You sit on your bench and I on the ground—Let us change places and then open the door . . . I have a cold already.

BUBNOFF (*undisturbed*). It is not for me . . . Your wife asks for it.

KLESHTSCH (*scowling*). A good many things are being asked for in this world.

SAHTIN. My headpiece hums. Ah, why do people always go for your head?

BUBNOFF. Not only the head, but also other parts of the body are often struck. (*Gets up.*) I must get some thread. Our housekeepers are late in showing themselves today. But they might be rotting already for all I know. (*Ex. L. U. E.* ANNA *coughs.* SAHTIN, *with his hands under his neck, lies motionless.*)

ACTOR (*regards the atmosphere with melancholy and goes to* ANNA's *bed*). Well, how is it? Bad?

ANNA. It is stifling . . .

ACTOR. Shall I take you out in the entry . . . Get up then. (*He helps the sick woman up, throws tattered shawl over her shoulders and supports her, as they totter up the steps to the landing.*) How, now . . . be steady. I, too, am a sick man—poisoned with alcohol. (*Enter* KOSTILIOFF. *L. U. E.*)

KOSTILIOFF (*at the door*). Out for promenade? What a fine couple—Jack and Jill.

ACTOR. Stand aside. Don't you see that—the sick are passing by?

KOSTILIOFF. All right, pass by, then. (*Humming the melody of a church hymn, he takes a mistrustful look about the basement, descends to the floor, leans his head to the left as if to overhear something in* PEPEL's *room.* KLESH-TSCH *claps furiously with the keys and files noisily, the proprietor giving him a black look.*) Busy scraping, eh? (*Crosses to R. F.*)

KLESHTSCH. What?

KOSTILIOFF. Busy scraping, I said . . . (*Pause.*) Hm—yes . . . What was I going to say? (*Hastily and in a lower tone.*) Wasn't my wife there?

KLESHTSCH. Haven't seen her . . .

KOSTILIOFF (*guardedly approaches the door of* PEPEL's *room*). How much space you take for your two rubles a month! That bed . . . You yourself sitting everlastingly here—nyah, five rubles worth, at least. I raise you half a ruble . . .

KLESHTSCH. Put a halter around my neck . . . and raise me a little more. You are an old man, you'll soon be rotting in your grave . . . and you think of nothing but half rubles.

KOSTILIOFF. Why should I halter you? Who would be the better for that? Live, may God bless you, be content. Yet I raise you half a ruble to buy oil for the holy lamps . . . and my offering will burn before the holy image . . . for the remission of my sins, and thine also . . . You never think yourself of your sins, I guess, do you . . . ah, Andreuschka, what a sinful beast you are . . . your wife languishing in agony from your blows . . . nobody likes you, nobody respects you . . . your work is so grating that nobody can endure you . . .

KLESHTSCH (*cries out*). Do you come . . . to hack me to pieces? (SAHTIN *roars aloud*.)

KOSTILIOFF (*shudders*). Ah . . . What is the matter with you, my friend!

ACTOR (*enters from stairs L. U. E.*). I took the woman into the entry . . . put her in a chair and wrapped her up warm . . .

KOSTILIOFF. What a good Samaritan you are. It will be rewarded . . .

ACTOR. When?

KOSTILIOFF. In the next world, brother dear . . . There they sit and reckon up our every word and deed.

ACTOR. Why not, for the goodness of my heart, give me some recompense here?

KOSTILIOFF. How can I do that?

ACTOR.   Knock off half my debt . . .

KOSTILIOFF.   Ha, ha, always having your fun, little buck, always jollying . . . Can goodness of the heart be ever repaid with money? Goodness of the heart stands higher than all the treasures of this world. Nyah. (*An expression equivalent to no or yes*)  and your debt—is only a debt . . . There it stands . . . Goodness of the heart you must bestow upon an old man without recompense . . .

ACTOR.   You are a cunning old knave . . . (*Ex. R. in kitchen.*)

(KLESCHTSCH *rises and goes up-stairs, L. U. E.*)

KOSTILIOFF (*to* SAHTIN).   Who just sneaked out? The scrape? He is not fond of me, he, he!

SAHTIN.   Who is fond of you except the devil?

KOSTILIOFF (*laughs quietly*).   Don't scold. I have you all so nicely . . . my dear friends, but I am fond of you all, my poor, unhappy brethren, citizens of nowhere, hapless and helpless . . . (*Suddenly brisk.*) Tell me . . . is Wasjka at home?

SAHTIN.   Look and see for yourself.

(KOSTILIOFF *goes to* PEPEL'*s door, L. U., and knocks*) . . . Wasjka! (*Enter* ACTOR *R. standing in kitchen door chewing something.*)

PEPEL (*within*).   Who's that?

KOSTILIOFF.   Me, Wasjka . . .

PEPEL (*within*).   What do you want? . . .

KOSTILIOFF (*stepping back*).   Open the door.

SAHTIN (*pretending to be oblivious*).   She is there. The moment he opens it . . . (*The* ACTOR *chuckles to him.*)

KOSTILIOFF (*disturbed, softly*).   How, who is in there? What . . .

SAHTIN. Hm? Do you speak to me?

KOSTILIOFF. What did you say?

SAHTIN. Nothing at all . . . only . . . to myself . . .

KOSTILIOFF. Take good care of yourself, my friend . . . you are too waggish. (*Knocks loudly on the door.*) Wassili . . .

PEPEL (*opening the door*). What are you bothering me about?

KOSTILIOFF (*peers into* PEPEL'S *room*). I . . . you see . . . you see. . . .

PEPEL. Have you brought the money?

KOSTILIOFF. I have a little business with you.

PEPEL. Have you brought the money?

KOSTILIOFF. Which money . . . wait.

PEPEL. Money, the seven rubles for the watch, see!

KOSTILIOFF. Which watch, Wasjka! Ah, you . . . none of your tricks.

PEPEL. Be careful. I sold you yesterday in the presence of witnesses a watch for ten rubles . . . I got three, and now I'll take the other seven. Out with them. What are you blinking about around here . . . disturbing everybody . . . and forgetting the main thing . . .

KOSTILIOFF. Ssh! Not so quick, Wasjka. The watch was, indeed . . .

SAHTIN. Stolen . . .

KOSTILIOFF (*stoutly, sharply*). I never receive stolen goods . . . How dare you . . .

PEPEL (*takes him by the shoulders*). Tell me, why did you wake me up? What do you want?

KOSTILIOFF. I . . . Nothing at all . . . I am going already . . . when you act so.

PEPEL. Go then, and bring me the money.

KOSTILIOFF (*as he goes*).   Tough customers . . . ah!
ah! (*Ex. L. U. E.*)

ACTOR.   Here is comedy for you!

SAHTIN.   Very good, I like it . . .

PEPEL.   What did he want?

SAHTIN (*laughing*).   Don't you catch on? He was looking for his wife . . . Say, why don't you do him, Wasjka?

PEPEL.   Would it pay to spoil my life for such stuff?

SAHTIN.   Spoil your life! Naturally you must do it
cleverly . . . Then marry Wassilissa . . . and be our
landlord . . .

PEPEL.   That would be nice. You, my guests, would
soon guzzle up the whole place, and me in the bargain
. . . I am much too open-handed for you. (*Sits on the
pritsche U.*)   Yes, old devil! Waked me up out of my
best sleep . . . I was having a beautiful dream. I dreamed
that I was fishing, and suddenly a big trout. A trout, I tell
you . . . only in dreams are there such great trout . . . I
pulled and pulled, till his gills almost snapped off . . . and
just as I was finishing him with a net . . . and thinking
I had him . . .

SAHTIN.   'Twasn't any trout, 'twas Wassilissa.

ACTOR.   He has had her in the net a long while.

PEPEL (*angrily*).   Go to the devil . . . with your Wassilissa.

KLESHTSCH (*entering L. U. E.*).   Keen as a knife, outside . . . wolf weather!

ACTOR.   Why didn't you bring Anna back? She will
freeze to death . . .

KLESHTSCH.   Natasha has taken her along to the
kitchen . . .

ACTOR.   The old scamp will chase her out . . .

KLESHTSCH (*crosses R. D. and sits down to work*). Natasha will soon bring her in.

SAHTIN. Wassili, five copecs.

ACTOR. Yes, five copecs, Wasjka, give us twenty . . .

PEPEL. If I don't hurry . . . You'll want a whole ruble . . . there! (*Gives the* ACTOR *a coin.*)

SAHTIN. Giblartarr! There are no better men in the world than the thieves!

KLESHTSCH. They get their money easy . . . they don't work . . .

SAHTIN. Money comes easy to many, but very few give it up easily . . . Work, if you arrange it so that work gives me joy, then perhaps I will work too . . . perhaps! When work is a pleasure—then life is beautiful . . . When you must work—then life is a slavery. (*To* ACTOR). Come Sardanapálus, we will go . . .

ACTOR. Come Nebuchadnézzar, I will get as drunk as forty thousand topers. (*Ex. both L. U. E.*)

PEPEL (*gapes*). How is your wife?

KLESHTSCH (*pause*). She won't last long, I guess.

PEPEL. When I sit and watch you so, I think, what good comes of all your scraping.

KLESHTSCH. What else shall I do?

PEPEL. Do nothing.

KLESHTSCH. How shall I eat?

PEPEL. Other men eat without taking so much trouble.

KLESHTSCH. Other men? You mean this ragged pack of tramps here, idlers, you call them men. I am a working-man . . . I am ashamed to look at them. I have worked from childhood on. Do you think that I shall never crawl out of this cesspool again? It is quite certain, let me work the skin off my hands, but I'll get out . . . wait until after my wife dies . . . six months in this hole . . . it seems like six years.

PEPEL.    What are you complaining about . . . we are no worse than you.

KLESHTSCH.    No worse . . . people living on God's earth without honor or conscience?

PEPEL (*in an impartial tone, cool*).    What good is honor or conscience? You can't put such things on your feet when the snow is on the ground. Honor and conscience to those in power and authority.

BUBNOFF (*enters L. U. E.*).    Ug-h! I'm frozen stiff.

PEPEL.    Tell me, Bubnoff, have you a conscience?

BUBNOFF.    What? A conscience?

PEPEL.    Yes.

BUBNOFF.    What use to me? I'm no millionaire . . .

PEPEL.    That's what I say. Honor and conscience are only for the rich—and yet Kleshtsch, here, is pulling us over the coals; we have no consciences, he says . . .

BUBNOFF.    Does he want to borrow some from us?

PEPEL.    He has plenty of his own . . .

BUBNOFF.    Maybe you'll sell us some? No, it don't sell here. If it was broken hat boxes, I'd buy . . . but only on credit . . .

PEPEL (*instructively, to* KLESHTSCH).    You're certainly a fool, Andreuschka. You ought to hear what Sahtin says about a conscience . . . or the Baron . . .

KLESHTSCH.    I have nothing to talk to them about . . .

PEPEL.    They have more wit than you, even if they are drunks . . .

BUBNOFF.    When a clever fellow drinks, he doubles his wit.

PEPEL.    Sahtin says: every man wants his neighbor to

have some conscience—but for himself, he can do without it . . . and that's right.

(NATASHA *enters L. U. E., and behind her* LUKA, *with a staff in his hand, a sack on his back, and a small kettle and tea boiler at his girdle.*)

LUKA. Good day to you, honest folks.

PEPEL (*pulling his moustache*). A-h, Natasha.

BUBNOFF (*to* LUKA). Honest were we once, as you must know, but since last spring, a year ago . . .

NATASHA. Here—a new lodger . . .

LUKA (*to* BUBNOFF). It's all the same to me. I know how to respect thieves, too. Any flea, say I, may be just as good as you or me; all are black, and all jump . . . that's the truth. Where shall I quarter myself here, my love?

NATASHA (*points to the kitchen door*). Go in there . . . daddy.

LUKA. Thank you, my girl, as you say . . . A warm corner is an old man's delight. (*Ex. R. into kitchen.*)

PEPEL. What an agreeable old chap you have brought along, Natasha.

NATASHA. No matter, he is more interesting than you. (*Then to* KLESHTSCH.) Andrew, your wife is with us in the kitchen . . . come for her after a while.

KLESHTSCH. All right, I'll come.

NATASHA. Be good to her now . . . we won't have her long . . .

KLESHTSCH. I know it . . .

NATASHA. Yes, you know it . . . but that is not enough! Make it quite clear to yourself, think what it means to die . . . it is frightful . . .

PEPEL. You see I am not afraid . . .

NATASHA. The brave are not . . .

BUBNOFF (*whistles*). The thread is rotten.

PEPEL. Certainly I am not afraid, I would welcome death right now. Take a knife and strike me in the heart —not a murmur will I utter. I would meet death with joy . . . from clean hands . . . like yours.

NATASHA (*as she goes*). Do not say anything which is not so, Pepel.

BUBNOFF (*drawing*). The thread is absolutely rotten.

NATASHA (*from the door to the entry*). Don't forget your wife, Andrew.

KLESHTSCH. All right. (*Ex.* NATASHA.)

PEPEL. A fine girl.

BUBNOFF. None better.

PEPEL. But what has set her against me so? She alone . . . always refusing me . . . but this life will be her ruin, all the same.

BUBNOFF. It is you who will be the ruin of her.

PEPEL. I be her ruin . . . I pity her . . .

BUBNOFF. As the wolf pities the lamb.

PEPEL. You lie! I do pity her . . . Her lot is very hard . . . I see that . . .

KLESHTSCH. Just wait until Wassilissa finds you together . . .

BUBNOFF. Yes, Wassilissa! Nobody can play any tricks on her, the fiend.

PEPEL (*stretches himself out on the pritsche, U.*) The devil take you both, prophets.

KLESHTSCH. Wait . . . and see . . .

LUKA (*within, singing*). 'In the darkness of midnight, no path can be found.'

KLESHTSCH. Now he begins to howl . . . (*crosses to L. U. E.*) He too. (*Ex.*)

PEPEL. My heart is in the depths . . . why it is? We live and live and everything goes well . . . then an unwarned moment comes . . . melancholy like a blighting frost settles upon us. Life is used up . . .

BUBNOFF. Sad, melancholy, eh? . . .

PEPEL. Yes . . . by God.

LUKA (*singing*). "No path can be found."

PEPEL. Heh, you bag of bones.

LUKA (*enters R.*). Do you mean me?

PEPEL. Yes, you. Cut the singing out.

LUKA (*crossing to C.*). Don't you like singing?

PEPEL. When singing is well sung, I enjoy it.

LUKA. Then I do not sing well?

PEPEL. That's about right.

LUKA. Too bad, and I thought that I sang beautifully. So it always goes. You think to yourself, I have done that well, but the public is not pleased . . .

PEPEL (*laughs*). You are right, there.

BUBNOFF. Ump! roaring again, and just now you said life was so sad, melancholy.

PEPEL. What have you to say about it, old raven . . .

LUKA. Who is despondent?

PEPEL. I . . . (*the* BARON *enters L. U. E.*).

LUKA. So, and there—in the kitchen sits a girl reading a book and crying; in truth! Her tears flowing . . . I asked her, what troubles you, my love—eh? And she said: It is so pitiful . . . Who do you pity then? I asked . . . See, here in the book, the people, said she . . . And that is how she passes her time to drive away despondency, it appears . . .

BARON. She is a fool.

PEPEL. Have you had your tea, Baron? (*an invitation.*)

BARON. Tea, yes . . . anything more?

PEPEL. Shall I stand for a bottle of rum, eh, that's right.

BARON. Of course . . . what more?

PEPEL. Let me ask you to stand on all fours and bark like a dog.

BARON. Blockhead; are you a Croesus? Or are you drunk?

PEPEL. So, bark away. I shall enjoy it . . . You are a gentleman . . . There was once a time when you did not take us for human beings even . . . and so on . . . and so on.

BARON. Well, and what more.

PEPEL. What more? I'll let you bark now. You wait?

BARON. I have no objection on my own account . . . booby. How can it be such fun for you . . . When I know myself that I am sunk deeper even than you . . . Had you once dared you ought to have tried to get me on all fours when I was above you.

BUBNOFF. You are right.

LUKA. So I say too, you are right.

BUBNOFF. What has been has been. Nothing is left but trash . . . we are not dukes here . . . the trappings are gone . . . only the bare man remains . . .

LUKA. All are alike, know that . . . Were you once a baron, my friend?

BARON. What's that you say? Who are you, sepulchre?

LUKA (*laughs*). An earl I have seen already, and a prince . . . too . . . But now for the first time, a baron, and a seedy one . . .

PEPEL (*laughs*). Ha, ha, ha, I blush for you, Baron.

BARON. Don't be an idiot, Wassili . . .

LUKA. Yes, yes, my friends. When I look around me . . . this life here . . . ah!

BUBNOFF. This life, . . . why, this life here would make any man howl, from break-o'-day on, like a starving owl.

BARON. To be sure, we have all seen better days. I for example . . . On waking up I used to drink my coffee in bed . . . coffee with cream . . . that's right.

LUKA. And you are still a man. No matter what somersaults you turn before us, as a man you were born and as a man you must die. The more I look about myself, the more I contemplate mankind, the more interesting he grows . . . poorer and poorer he sinks and higher and higher his aspirations mount . . . obstinacy.

BARON. Tell me, old man . . . exactly who you are . . . where do you come from?

LUKA. Who? I?

BARON. Are you a pilgrim?

LUKA. We are all pilgrims here on this earth . . . It has been said, even, I am told, that our earth is only a pilgrimage to Heaven's gate . . .

BARON. It is so, but tell me . . . have you a passport?

LUKA (*hesitatingly*). Who are you? A secret police?

PEPEL (*briskly*). Well said, old man! Ha, my lord, that went home!

BUBNOFF. He gets what is coming to him . . .

BARON (*disconcerted*). Well! well- I am only joking, old man. I've no papers, myself.

BUBNOFF. You lie!

BARON. That is to say . . . I have papers . . . but all to no purpose.

LUKA.   So it is with all pen scratches . . . all to no purpose . . .

PEPEL.   Baron! Come have one, for the sake of thirst . . .

BARON.   I'm with you. Bye-bye, see you again, old chap . . . sly dog . . .

LUKA.   It may be true, my friend.

PEPEL (*at the door L. U. E.*).   Are you coming? (*Ex. followed quickly by the* BARON.)

LUKA.   Has the man really been a baron?

BUBNOFF.   Who knows? He has been a nobleman, that is certain. Even yet his former air shows through. The manner clings . . .

LUKA.   Breeding is like the smallpox: The man recovers, but the pits remain.

BUBNOFF.   But otherwise he is a good fellow . . . except that sometimes he is overbearing . . . As he was about your passport . . .

ALYOSCHKA (*enters L. U. E. drunk, an accordion under his arm. He whistles*).   Hey, there, neighbors.

BUBNOFF.   What are you howling about?

ALYOSCHKA.   Excuse me, please . . . pass it over. I am a cozy boy . . .

BUBNOFF.   Broken out again?

ALYOSCHKA.   Why not? Police Captain Medviskin has just chased me off his beat. "Take your stand out of the street," says he. No, no, I am still a youth of good temperament . . . the boss was jawing at me too . . . bah, what do I care for bosses . . . bah, everything is all a mistake, should a tank be boss . . . I am a man, who . . . never a wish have . . . has . . . I want nothing . . . that settles it . . . now, take me . . . for one ruble and twenty copecs you can have me . . . and I want ab-solt-ly nothing. (NASTIAH *enters R. from kitchen.*) Offer me a million—and I will not take it. And that whisky barrel, to be boss over me, a good man, no better than—it don't go. I'll not stand for it. (NASTIAH *remains standing at the door, shaking her head at the spectacle of* ALYOSCHKA.)

LUKA (*good-naturedly*). Ah, boy . . . you can't unravel it.

BUBNOFF. There you have human folly.

ALYOSCHKA (*lies down on the floor*). Now, eat me up. Costs nothing. I am a desperado. You just tell me, am I worse than the others? How am I worse? Just think, Medviskin said: "Don't show yourself on the street, or else I'll give you one in the snout." But I'll go . . . I'll lie down crosswise in the street, let them choke me. I want ab-solt-ly nothing . . . (*rises*).

NASTIAH. Wretch . . . so young and putting on such airs . . .

ALYOSCHKA (*sees her, and kneels*). My lady, my fraulein, mamsell! Parlez français . . . price current . . . I am jagging.

NASTIAH (*whispers loudly*). Wassilissa. (*Sees her coming.*)

WASSILISSA (*opens door at head of stairs R. U. E. to* ALYOSCHKA). Here again, . . . already?

ALYOSCHKA. Good morning. Please, come down.

WASSILISSA. Didn't I tell you, you pup, not to show yourself here again? (*Descends.*)

ALYOSCHKA. Wassilissa Karpovna—if you please, I'll play you a funeral march.

WASSILISSA (*pushes him on the shoulder*). Get out!

ALYOSCHKA (*shuffles to the door, L. U. E.*). No, not so,

wait. First the funeral march . . . I've just learned it . . . new music . . . wait a minute . . . you must not act so.

WASSILISSA.    I will show you how I must act . . . I'll put the whole street on your track, you damned heathen . . . so, telling folks on me . . .

ALYOSCHKA (*runs out L. U. E.*).    No, I am already gone. (*Ex.*)

WASSILISSA (*to* BUBNOFF).    See to it that he does not set foot in here again, you hear?

BUBNOFF.    I'm not your watchman.

WASSILISSA.    No, but you are a dead beat. How much do you owe me?

BUBNOFF (*calmly*).    I haven't counted it up. . . .

WASSILISSA.    Look out or I'll count it up.

ALYOSCHKA (*opens the door and cries*).    Wassilissa Karpovna, I am not afraid of you . . . I am not afraid. (*He hides behind a cloth which hangs over the balustrade and* LUKA *laughs.*)

WASSILISSA.    And who are you?

LUKA.    A pilgrim, a mere wanderer. I go from place to place . . .

WASSILISSA.    Will you stay over night . . . or permanent?

LUKA.    I will see (ALYOSCHKA *slips into the kitchen*).

WASSILISSA.    Your passport.

LUKA.    You may have it.

WASSILISSA.    Give it to me, then.

LUKA.    I'll get it presently . . . I'll drag it to your room . . .

WASSILISSA.    A pilgrim . . . You look it; say a vagabond . . . that sounds more like the truth . . .

LUKA (*sighs*).  You are not very hospitable, mother. (WASSILISSA *goes to* PEPEL'*s door.*)

ALYOSCHKA (*whispers, from the kitchen*).  Has she gone? . . . hm.

WASSILISSA (*turns on him*).  Are you still there? (ALYOSCHKA *disappears into the kitchen, whistling.* NASTIAH *and* LUKA *laugh.*)

BUBNOFF (*to* WASSILISSA).  He is not there . . .

WASSILISSA.  Who?

BUBNOFF.  Wasjka. (ALYOSCHKA *slips around to the stairs, Ex. L. U. E.*)

WASSILISSA.  Have I asked you for him?

BUBNOFF.  I can see that you are looking into every corner.

WASSILISSA.  I am looking after things, do you understand.  Why have you not swept up?  How often have I told you that you must keep the place clean?

BUBNOFF.  It's the actor's turn today . . .

WASSILISSA.  It makes no difference to me whose turn it is.  When the Health Department people come and fine me, I'll have you thrown out . . .

BUBNOFF (*calmly*).  And what will you live off of then?

WASSILISSA.  See that not a speck of dust is left. (*Goes to the kitchen door to* NASTIAH.)  And what are you standing around like a post for?  What are they gawking about?  Sweep up!  Have you not seen . . . Natalya?  Has she been here?

NASTIAH.  I don't know . . . I haven't seen her.

WASSILISSA.  Bubnoff, was my sister here?

BUBNOFF.  Certainly.  She brought the old man.

WASSILISSA.  And he, was he in his room?

BUBNOFF. Wassili . . . to be sure . . . She was talking with Kleschtsch . . . Natalya . . .

WASSILISSA. I did not ask you who she was talking with . . . Dirt everywhere, a foot thick. Ah, you pigs. See that you clean up . . . do you hear me? (*Exit quickly R. U. E.*)

BUBNOFF. What an awful lot of bitterness that woman has.

LUKA. A brutal wife.

NASTIAH. This life would brutalize anybody. And tied to such a husband—how can that be endured?

BUBNOFF. She does not feel tied, so very tight . . .

LUKA. Is she always . . . so biting?

BUBNOFF. Always . . . she was looking for her lover, you see, and that dismayed her.

LUKA. Um, so that's the trouble . . . ah, yes, how many different people there are here on this earth go bossing around . . . and all trying to lord it over the rest, but in spite of it all bringing no cleanness about.

BUBNOFF. They try, indeed, to bring order about, but the wit is lacking . . . which means, that we must finally clean up . . . Nastiah . . . won't you do it?

NASTIAH. Certainly! Am I your chambermaid? (*She remains silent for a time.*) I'll get drunk today . . . soaked full. (*Motion of her hand to her chin.*)

BUBNOFF. Good business.

LUKA. What are you going to get drunk for, my daughter. You were crying a moment ago, and now you promise to get drunk . . .

NASTIAH (*defiantly*). And when I have gotten drunk, I will cry again . . . that's all . . .

BUBNOFF. But it's not much.

LUKA. For what reason, tell me? Everything has a cause, even the smallest pimple in the face. (NASTIAH *is silent, shaking her head.*)

LUKA. Aye, aye, such is man . . . that's the way with people, what will become of them? I will sweep up myself. Where do you keep the broom?

BUBNOFF. In the entry, behind the door. (*Ex.* LUKA *L. U. E.*) Tell me, Nastenka.

NASTIAH (*sits R. U. before stove*). Um.

BUBNOFF. What has Wassilissa got against Alyoschka, so much?

NASTIAH. He has told everybody that Waska don't like her any more . . . is tired of her, is going to give her up, for Natasha interests him . . . I am going to pull out and find another place . . .

BUBNOFF. Why so?

NASTIAH. I am tired of it. I am in the way . . . superfluous.

BUBNOFF (*thoughtfully*). Where wouldn't you be superfluous? Everybody here on earth is superfluous . . . (NASTIAH *shakes her head, rises and goes quietly up-stairs R. U. E.* MEDVIÉDEFF *enters L. U. E. followed by* LUKA *with the broom.*)

MEDVIÉDEFF (*to* LUKA). I don't remember having seen you.

LUKA. And the rest, you've seen them. Do you know everybody?

MEDVIÉDEFF. Along my beat I must know everybody— and I don't know you . . .

LUKA. You would, if your beat included the whole world, but there is a small corner which has been left off. (*Ex. R.*)

MEDVIÉDEFF (*crossing to* BUBNOFF *L.*). That's right. My beat is not large . . . but the work is worse than in lots bigger ones. Just as I came off duty I had to take that young cobbler Alyoschka to the station house. The rascal was sprawled out on his back in the middle of the street, if you can believe it, playing his accordion and bellowing: 'I want for nothing, I wish for nothing,' and wagons coming both ways and traffic everywhere . . . He could easily have been run over, or something else happen . . . rattle-brain . . . Of course I locked him up . . . he is a little too fresh.

BUBNOFF. Come around tonight . . . We'll have a game of checkers.

MEDVIÉDEFF. I'll come . . . hm, yes . . . but how is it about Waska?

BUBNOFF. All right . . . Same old thing . . .

MEDVIÉDEFF. Still alive.

BUBNOFF. Why not, his life is worth living.

MEDVIÉDEFF (*doubtfully*). So . . . has he? (LUKA *enters R. from kitchen, and Ex. L. U. E., a bucket in his hand.*) Hm—yes . . . there is a rumor about . . . Waska . . . haven't you heard?

BUBNOFF. I've heard lots of things.

MEDVIÉDEFF. Something about Wassilissa, he . . . have you not noticed?

BUBNOFF. What?

MEDVIÉDEFF. So . . . in general . . . you know all about it but don't like to say so . . . it is well known . . . (*strongly*) don't lie, my friend!

BUBNOFF. Why should I lie?

MEDVIÉDEFF. I thought . . . ah, the curs . . . they

say, in short that Waska with Wassilissa . . . so to speak
. . . nyah, what do I care? I am not her father, but only
. . . her uncle . . . It can't hurt me if they can't laugh at
me. (KVASCHNYA *enters L. U. E.*). A bad lot . . .ah, you
have come . . .

KVASCHNYA. My dear captain. Just think, Bubnoff, he
proposed to me again at the market . . .

BUBNOFF. What of it . . . Why do you put him off?
He has money, and is a pretty hearty lover, even yet . . .

MEDVIÉDEFF. I, . . . to be sure.

KVASCHNYA. Ah, you old grey stud-horse. No, don't
come near it. That foolishness happens to me only once
in a lifetime, and I've been through it already. Marriage,
for a woman, is like jumping into the river in winter; once
she's done it, she remembers it all her life.

MEDVIÉDEFF. Wait . . . the husbands are not all the
same . . .

KVASCHNYA. But I always remain the same. When my
dear husband—when the devil took him—when he became
a carcass, damn his ghost, I did not leave the house the
whole day for joy; I sat there all alone and could scarcely
believe my happiness.

MEDVIÉDEFF. Why did you allow your husband to beat
you? If you had gone to the police . . .

KVASCHNYA. Police! I complained to God for eight
years . . . and even God couldn't do anything.

MEDVIÉDEFF. But it is illegal now to beat wives . . .
Law and order are now enforced . . . No man dare beat
anybody now, except for the sake of law and order . . .
Wife beating happens only in lawless places . . .

LUKA (*leads* ANNA *in, L. U. E.*). Now, look out . . .

now we've crawled down . . . ah, you poor child . . . How could you go around alone so, in your condition? Where is your quarter?

ANNA (*draws toward L. D.*). Thank you, daddy.

KVASCHNYA. There you have a married woman . . . look at her.

LUKA. Such a poor, weak thing . . . creeping about quite alone there up in the entry, clinging to the walls—moaning without cease . . . why did you allow her to go out alone?

KVASCHNYA. We did not notice it—pardon me, grandfather. Her lady in waiting has probably gone for a stroll . . .

LUKA. So you laugh . . . How can you abandon another so? Whatever he may have become—he still remains a human being.

MEDVIÉDEFF. This ought to be investigated. If she dies suddenly? We shall be mixed up in it. Give her every attention.

LUKA. Quite right, Mr. Captain . . .

MEDVIÉDEFF. Hm . . . yes . . . you may say so . . . though I'm not a captain yet . . .

LUKA. Is it possible? But we should conclude from your appearance that you are a true hero. (*From above a noise, the stamping of feet and smothered cries.*)

MEDVIÉDEFF. Not quite yet—looks like a row.

BUBNOFF. It sounds like one . . .

KVASCHNYA. I'll go see.

MEDVIÉDEFF. And I've got to go too . . . ah, the service! Why should people be pulled apart when they brawl? But they finally quit fighting of their own accord . . . when they are tired of thumping each other . . . the best thing to do is to let them get their bellies full of fighting . . . then they don't row so often . . . they aren't in shape to . . .

BUBNOFF (*gets off his bench*).   You must lay your plan before the authorities . . .

KOSTILIOFF (*throws open the door L. U. E. and cries*). Abram . . . come . . . quick . . . Wassilissa kills Natasha . . . come . . . come!

(KVASCHNYA, MEDVIÉDEFF, BUBNOFF *run to the entry, L. U. E., and* LUKA *looks after them, shaking his head.*)

ANNA.   Ah, God . . . the poor Natashenka!

LUKA.   Who is brawling there?

ANNA.   Our landlady . . . the two sisters . . .

LUKA (*approaches* ANNA).   Over heirlooms.

ANNA.   Both are well fed . . . both are healthy . . .

LUKA.   And you . . . what is your name?

ANNA.   Anna, I am called . . . When I look at you . . . you are so much like my father, just like my own dear father . . . you, too, are so kind and tender . . .

LUKA.   Because they have knocked me about the world so much, that is why I am tender. (*Chuckles to himself.*)

# ACT II

(*The same scene. Evening.* SAHTIN, THE BARON, KRIVOI
ZOBA *and the* TARTAR *are sitting on the pritsche before
the stove, playing cards.* KLESHTSCH *and the* ACTOR *are
watching the game.* BUBNOFF *on his bench is playing Parti-
Dame with* MEDVIÉDEFF. LUKA *is sitting on the tabouret at*
ANNA's *bed. The room is lit by two lamps, one hanging on
the wall over the card players on the right and the other
above* BUBNOFF's *bench.*

TARTAR. I'll play one more game . . . and then I
quit . . .

BUBNOFF. Krivoi Zoba! A song. (*He sings.*) 'Though
still the sun goes up and down.'

KRIVOI ZOBA (*falling in*). 'No gleam can pierce to me
in here . . .'

TARTAR (*to* SAHTIN). Shuffle the cards, but no
crooked business. We already know what a swindler you
are.

BUBNOFF *and* KRIVOI ZOBA (*sing together.*)
'By day and night my guards stand watch—a—ach,
My Prison window always near . . .'

ANNA. Illness and blows . . . I have endured . . .
they have been my lot . . . my whole life long.

LUKA. Ah, you poor child! Do not grieve.

38

MEDVIÉDEFF. What nerve! Be careful!

BUBNOFF. Ah, ha! So . . . and so, and so . . . (*throws down card after card*).

TARTAR (*threatens* SAHTIN *with his fist*). What are you hiding the cards for! I saw you . . . you.

KRIVOI ZOBA. Let him go, Hassan. They're bound to cheat us, one way or another . . . Sing some more, Bubnoff.

ANNA. I cannot remember to have ever had enough to eat . . . with trembling and fear . . . have I eaten every piece of bread . . . I have trembled and constantly feared . . . lest I eat more than my share . . . My whole life long have I gone in rags . . . my whole ill-fated life . . . Why should this have been?

LUKA. Ah, you poor child! You are tired? It will soon be right!

ACTOR (*to* KRIVOI ZOBA). Play the jack . . . the jack, damn it.

BARON. And we have the king!

KLESHTSCH. These cards will always win.

SAHTIN. So . . . they will.

MEDVIÉDEFF. A queen!

BUBNOFF. Another . . . there!

ANNA. I am dying . . .

KLESHTSCH (*to the* TARTAR). There—look out! Throw the cards down, prince, stop playing.

ACTOR. Don't you think he knows what to do?

BARON. Be careful, Andrejuschka, that I don't throw you out the door.

TARTAR. Again, I say. The pitcher goes to the well, then it breaks . . . the same with me . . . (KLESHTSCH *shakes his head and goes behind* BUBNOFF.)

ANNA.  I am always thinking to myself: My Saviour
. . . shall I there too . . . in that world . . . endure such
tortures?

LUKA.  No! Never! . . . You will suffer nothing. Lie
perfectly still . . . and have no fear. You shall find peace
there! Be patient yet a little while . . . We must all suffer,
my love . . . Every one endures life in his own way. (*He
rises and goes hastily into the kitchen R.*)

BUBNOFF.  'Spy on, with the might of your eyes, forever.'

KRIVOI ZOBA.  'On freedom still my thoughts shall
dwell . . .'

TOGETHER.  'I cannot spring these chains and locks—a—
ach . . . Nor fly the walls of this cold cell . . .'

TARTAR.  Stop! He has pushed a card up his sleeve.

BARON (*confused*).  No, where else then?

ACTOR (*convincingly*).  You have made a mistake,
prince! It's not to be thought of . . .

TARTAR.  I saw it! Cheats! I play no more!

SAHTIN (*throwing the cards together*).  Then go your
way, Hassan . . . You know that we are cheats—so why
did you play with us?

BARON.  He's lost forty copecs, you'd think from the row
that he'd lost three hundred. And this is a prince!

TARTAR (*violently*).  Everybody must play fair!

SAHTIN.  But why, then?

TARTAR.  What does 'why' mean?

SAHTIN.  Only, so . . . why?

TARTAR.  Um, you don't know?

SAHTIN.  I don't know, do you?

TARTAR (*spits angrily, all laugh at him*).

KRIVOI ZOBA (*cheerfully*).  You are a comical owl,

Hassan. Think it over. If they lived honestly they would starve in three days . . .

TARTAR. What's that to me? People must live honestly.

KRIVOI ZOBA. Same old story, I'd rather have a drink of tea . . . cut loose, Bubnoff.

BUBNOFF. 'Alas, these heavy chains of iron, this armed patrol on ceaseless guard . . .'

KRIVOI ZOBA. Come, Hassan. (*Ex. singing*). 'No, nevermore shall I break through.' (*The* TARTAR *threatens the* BARON *with his fist, and then follows his comrade, Ex. R.*)

SAHTIN (*to the* BARON, *laughing*). Nyah, your worship, you've launched us triumphantly into the mire. You, an educated man, and can't handle cards . . .

BARON (*throwing up his hands*). The devil knows how the cards should be handled.

ACTOR. No genius, no self-confidence . . . without that you'll never be any good . . .

MEDVIÉDEFF. I have a queen, and you have two, hm, yes.

BUBNOFF. One is enough, if well played . . . your play.

KLESHTSCH. The game is lost, Abram Ivanitsch.

MEDVIÉDEFF. That is none of your business—understand? Hold your mouth . . .

SAHTIN. Fifty-three copecs won . . .

ACTOR. The three copecs are for me . . . though what do I want with three copecs?

LUKA (*entering from kitchen R.*). You soaked the Tartar dry. Are you going for some?

BARON. Come with us!

SAHTIN. I'd like to see you once after you've put a couple of dozen away . . .

LUKA. Surely I wouldn't look better than I do sober . . .

ACTOR. Come, old fellow . . . I will declaim for you a pair of pretty couplets . . .

LUKA. Couplets? What are they?

ACTOR. Verses, don't you understand . . .

LUKA. Verses, for me . . . poems? What do I want them for?

ACTOR. Ah, they are so comical . . . yet sometimes so sad . . .

SAHTIN. Are you coming, couplet singer? (*Ex. L. U. E. with the* BARON).

ACTOR. I will overtake you. (*To* LUKA). There is, old man, for example, a poem beginning . . . I have completely forgotten it . . . (*rubs his forehead*).

BUBNOFF. Your queen is lost . . . go.

MEDVIÉDEFF. I played wrong, the devil take it.

ACTOR. In the past, while my organism still was not yet poisoned with alcohol, I had a splendid memory . . . yes, patriarch! Now . . . it is all at an end with me . . . time and time again, with the greatest success I have recited this poem . . . to thundering applause . . . Do you know what applause means, brother, it is the wine of wines . . . when I came out, in this posture (*assumes an attitude*) and then began . . . and . . . (*he is silent*) no more . . . not a word . . . have I retained. And the poem was my heart's delight . . . Is that not frightful, patriarch (*clutches the air*).

LUKA. Alas, too bad . . . when the best beloved has been forgotten. In that which man loves, he finds his soul . . .

ACTOR. I have drowned my soul, patriarch . . . I am

a lost man . . . And why am I lost? Because I believe in myself no more . . . I am through . . .

LUKA.   Why so then. Be cured! The drunkard, I have heard, can now be cured. Without expense, my brother . . . A dispensary has been erected . . . there you may be cured without charge. They realize now, you see, that the drunkard is also a man, and they are glad when one comes to allow himself to be cured. Hurry, then, go there . . .

ACTOR (*thoughtfully*).   Where to? Where is it?

LUKA.   In a certain city . . . what is it called? A strange name . . . No, I can't tell you right now . . . but listen to me: You must begin to get ready! Be abstemious! Hold yourself together, and suffer, endure thus, . . . and then you'll be cured. Begin a new life . . . is that not splendid, brother: a new life . . . now, decide . . . one, two, three!

ACTOR (*smiling*).   A new life . . . from the start . . . that is beautiful . . . Can it be true? A new life? (*laughs*). Nyah . . . yes! I can! I can!

LUKA.   Why not? Man can achieve everything . . . if he only will . . .

ACTOR (*suddenly, as if awakened from a dream*). You're a queer customer! So long! See you again. (*He whistles.*)   Meantime, old man. (*Ex. L. U. E.*)

ANNA.   Daddy.

LUKA.   What is it, little mother?

ANNA.   Talk a little bit, to me . . .

LUKA (*going to her*).   Gladly . . . Let us have a long chat. (KLESHTSCH *looks around, silently goes to the bed of his wife, looks at her, gesticulates, as if about to speak.*)

LUKA.   Well, brother?

KLESHTSCH (*whispers as if in fear*).   Nothing. (*Goes*

*slowly to door, L. U. E. Remains a few moments, then goes out.*)

LUKA (*following him with his eyes*). Thy husband seems to be oppressed.

ANNA. I cannot think of him any more.

LUKA. Has he beaten you?

ANNA. How often . . . He has brought me . . . to this.

BUBNOFF. My wife . . . had once an admirer. He played with kings and queens quite splendidly, the rascal . . .

MEDVIÉDEFF. Hm.

ANNA. Grandfather . . . Talk to me, my dear . . . I am lonely . . .

LUKA. That is nothing. That may be felt before death, my dove. It means nothing, dear. Have faith. You will die, you see, and then enter into rest. Have fear of nothing more, of nothing more. It will be still, and peaceful . . . and you will lie resting there. Death subdues everything . . . he is so tender with us . . . Only in death shall rest be found, they say . . . and such is the truth, my love! Where shall rest be found here?

(PEPEL *enters L. U. E. a little drunk, dishevelled and sullen. He sits on the bunk by the kitchen door, silent and motionless.*)

ANNA. And shall there be such torture there?

LUKA. Nothing is there! Believe me, nothing! Rest alone—nothing else. They will lead you before the Master and will say: Look, oh, Master—thy servant Anna is come . . .

MEDVIÉDEFF (*vigorously*). How can you know what

shall be said there: have you ever heard . . . (PEPEL, *at the sound of* MEDVIÉDEFF'S *voice, raises his head and listens.*)

LUKA. My information is reliable, Mr. Commissioner . . .

MEDVIÉDEFF (*softly*). Hm—yes. Nyah, it is your affair . . . that means . . . but I am not a commissioner . . .

BUBNOFF. Two birds with one stone . . .

MEDVIÉDEFF. Ah, you, the devil take you . . .

LUKA. And the Master will look upon you in loving kindness and will say: 'I know this Anna!' 'Now,' he will say, 'lead her forth into Paradise. May she there find peace . . . I know her life was wearisome . . . she is very tired . . . let her have rest, our Anna.'

ANNA. Grandfather . . . you, my dear . . . if it is only so . . . if I there . . . find peace . . . and feel nothing more . . . suffer . . .

LUKA. You will suffer nothing . . . nothing! Only have faith! Die joyfully, without anxiety . . . Death to us, I say unto you, is like a mother soothing her children . . .

ANNA. But . . . perhaps . . . I will get well again?

LUKA (*laughing*). For what? To fresh tortures.

ANNA. But I might still . . . live a little while . . . a very little while . . . if there is no torture beyond . . . I can afford to suffer at the end here a little more . . .

LUKA. There shall be no more pain . . . none at all . . .

PEPEL (*rising*). True—it may be, and may not be!

ANNA. Ah, God . . .

LUKA. Ah, my dear boy . . .

MEDVIÉDEFF. Who is howling there?

PEPEL (*going to him*). Me, what's the matter?

MEDVIÉDEFF. People must keep quiet in here . . . You are howling without cause.

PEPEL. Ah . . . blockhead! And you her uncle . . . ha, ha!

LUKA (*whispers to* PEPEL). Listen, boy—not so loud. A woman is dying here . . . Her lips are covered with earth already . . . don't disturb her . . .

PEPEL. As you say so, grandfather, I will listen to you. You are a splendid chap, pilgrim . . . tell them famously . . . full of nice stories. Keep it up, brother, keep it up . . . there is so little pleasure in the world.

BUBNOFF. Is she dying for keeps?

LUKA. I guess she is not fooling.

BUBNOFF. Then we will finally be rid of that coughing . . . a great nuisance, her everlasting coughing . . . I take two . . .

MEDVIÉDEFF. Ah, . . . the devil take you.

PEPEL. Abram . . .

MEDVIÉDEFF. I am not Abram . . . for you . . .

PEPEL. Abrashka, tell me—is Natasha still sick?

MEDVIÉDEFF. Does that concern you?

PEPEL. No, but say: did Wassilissa really beat her up so badly?

MEDVIÉDEFF. And that's none of your business either . . . that's a family affair . . . who are you, anyhow, eh?

PEPEL. I may be who I am—but when it suits me, I will take your Natasha away. You will not see her again.

MEDVIÉDEFF (*interrupting his playing*). What do you say? Whom are you talking about? My niece shall . . . ach, you thief!

PEPEL. A thief—which you have not yet caught . . .

MEDVIÉDEFF.  Wait! I'll soon catch you . . . in a very little while I will have you . . .

PEPEL.  Whenever it suits you . . . and then your whole nest here will be torn up. Do you think I'll hold my tongue when it comes to the coroner? There you're badly mistaken. Who incited you to theft, they will ask—who put the opportunity before you? Mischka Kostilioff and his wife. And who received the stolen goods? Mischka Kostilioff and his wife.

MEDVIÉDEFF.  You lie! Nobody will believe it.

PEPEL.  They will quickly believe—because it is the truth. And I'll get you into the muddle too, and the rest of you, you gang of thieves—we shall soon see.

MEDVIÉDEFF (*uneasily*).  Shut up! Shut up! What have I done to you . . . you mad dog . . .

PEPEL.  What good have you done me?

LUKA.  Quite right . . .

MEDVIÉDEFF (*to* LUKA).  What are you croaking about? What business is this of yours? This is a family affair . . .

BUBNOFF (*to* LUKA).  Let them have it out . . . We two won't be haltered anyhow . . .

LUKA (*softly*).  I have done no harm. I only think that if a man does not do another good—then he has done wrong.

MEDVIÉDEFF (*who does not understand* LUKA).  Look, you. We are all acquainted here . . . And you—who are you? (*Ex. quickly L. U. E. angrily fuming.*)

LUKA.  He has gone mad, Sir Cavalier . . . oho! Very peculiar, brothers, what we have here, somewhat complicated.

PEPEL.  He has gone to Wassilissa, now, with it.

BUBNOFF.  Don't make a fool of yourself, Wassili. Don't

try to be the bravest. Bravery, my boy, is good, when you go into the woods for mushrooms . . . It is out of place here, . . . they have you by the throat . . . in a jiffy.

PEPEL. We shall see . . . We Yaroslavs are much too sly . . . we cannot be caught with the bare hands . . . will you have a fight . . . good, then we begin it . . .

LUKA. It would indeed, be better, boy, to go away . . .

PEPEL. Where then? Tell me . . .

LUKA. Go . . . to Siberia.

PEPEL. Ha! Ha! Never; I'll wait, rather, until they send me, at the expense of the government . . .

LUKA. No, really, listen to me! Go there; you can make your way in Siberia . . . they need such young fellows . . .

PEPEL. My way is already pointed out! My father spent his life in prison, and that fate is my legacy . . . when I was still a small boy they called me a thief and the son of a thief.

LUKA. A beautiful country, Siberia. A golden land. A man with strength and a clear head develops there . . . like a cucumber in a hot bed.

PEPEL. Tell me, pilgrim, why do you fabricate so ceaselessly?

LUKA. How?

PEPEL. Are you deaf? Why do you lie, I ask . . .

LUKA. When have I lied?

PEPEL. Right straight along . . . It is beautiful there, by your way of thinking, and beautiful here . . . which is not true. Why then, do you lie?

LUKA. Believe me! Or go there and convince yourself . . . You will send me thanks . . . why loiter here? And, whence comes your eagerness for truth? Think it over: the truth is, they may make an end of you here.

PEPEL. It is all the same . . . even a halter.

LUKA. You are a strange fellow. Why will you put your head into it?

BUBNOFF. What are you two jawing about? I don't catch on . . . What kind of truth do you want, Waska? What good would it be to you? You know the truth about yourself . . . and all the world knows it . . .

PEPEL. Hold your snout. Don't croak. He shall tell me first . . . hear, pilgrim . . . is there a God? (LUKA *laughs and remains silent.*)

BUBNOFF. Mankind is like chips which the storm sweeps away . . . the finished house remains, but the chips are gone.

LUKA (*softly*). If you believe in him, there is a God; believe not and none exists . . . What you believe in . . . exists . . . (PEPEL *looks silently surprised at the old man.*)

BUBNOFF. I'll have a drink of tea now . . . come with me to the ale house.

LUKA (*to* PEPEL). What are you staring at?

PEPEL. It means then . . . just so . . . wait . . .

BUBNOFF. Nyah, then I'll go alone. (*Ex. L. U. E., bumping into Wassilissa.*)

PEPEL. Then . . . do as you . . . then you . . .

WASSILISSA (*to* BUBNOFF). Is Nastassja at home?

BUBNOFF. No . . . (*Ex. L. U. E.*)

PEPEL. Ah . . . there she is.

WASSILISSA (*goes to* ANNA'*s bed*). Is she still alive?

LUKA. Do not disturb her.

WASSILISSA. And you, what are you loafing around for?

LUKA. I can go out, if I must . . .

WASSILISSA (*approaching* PEPEL'*s door*). Wassili! I have business with you . . . (LUKA *goes to the door,*

*L. U. E., opens it, closes it noisily, then carefully climbs up the stove and conceals himself.* WASSILISSA *has entered* PEPEL's *room. Within.*) Waska, come here.

PEPEL. I will not come . . . I will not . . .

WASSILISSA (*re-enters*). What's the matter? Why are you so mad?

PEPEL. It is tiresome . . . I am sick of the whole mess here . . .

WASSILISSA. And of me . . . are you also sick?

PEPEL. Also of you . . . (WASSILISSA *pulls the shawl which is over her shoulders closely together and presses her arm against her breast. She goes to* ANNA's *bed, looks cautiously behind the curtain, and returns to* PEPEL.) Nyah, so . . . speak . . .

WASSILISSA. What shall I say? No one can be forced to love . . . and I should be unlike myself to beg for love . . . for your frankness many thanks . . .

PEPEL. My frankness.

WASSILISSA. Yes, you say you are sick of me . . . or is it not true? (PEPEL *looks at her in silence. She approaches him.*) Why do you stare? Do you not know me? (WASSILISSA *puts her arm around his neck: he shakes it off with a movement of the shoulder.*) But still my heart has never belonged to you . . . I have gone on living with you . . . but I have never truly liked you . . .

WASSILISSA (*softly*). So . . . o . . . now . . . um . . .

PEPEL. Now we have nothing more to talk about . . . Nothing more . . . go away . . . leave me alone.

WASSILISSA. Have you found pleasure in another?

PEPEL. That is nothing to you . . . If it were so—I would not take you along for a matchmaker . . .

WASSILISSA (*meaningly*). Who knows . . . perhaps I can bring it about.

PEPEL (*suspiciously*). Who with?

WASSILISSA. You know who I mean . . . don't deny it . . . I talk straight out from the shoulder . . . (*softly*) I will only say . . . you have deeply wronged me . . . without provocation you have struck me a blow, as with a club . . . you always said you loved me, and . . . all of a sudden . . .

PEPEL. All of a sudden . . . not at all . . . I have thought so, long . . . you have no soul . . . In a woman there should be a soul. We men are animals . . . we know nothing else . . . and men must first be taught goodness . . . and you, what good have you taught me?

WASSILISSA. What has been has been . . . I know that we cannot control the impulses of our hearts . . . if you love me no more—good . . . it is all the same to me.

PEPEL. All right, then. It is settled. We separate in friendship, without scandal . . . pleasantly!

WASSILISSA. Stop, not so quick. During the whole time that we have lived together . . . I have always hoped you would help me out of this cesspool here . . . that you would free me from my husband, from my uncle . . . from this whole life . . . and perhaps I have not loved you, Waska, at all . . . perhaps in you I love only . . . my one hope, my one dream . . . do you understand? I had hoped you would pull me out . . .

PEPEL. You are no nail and I am no tongs . . . I had thought you would finish him; with your slyness . . . for you are sly and quick-witted . . . (*sits at R. table.*)

WASSILISSA (*leans toward him*). Waska, we will help each other . . .

PEPEL. How then?

WASSILISSA (*in a low tone, with expression*). My sister . . . you have taken a fancy to her, I know it . . .

PEPEL. And you knock her about so brutally on that account. I'll say this to you, Waska: don't touch her again.

WASSILISSA. Wait. Not so hotly. It can all be done quietly, in friendliness . . . Marry her whenever you feel like it. I'll find the money, three hundred rubles. If I can get more I'll give you more . . .

PEPEL (*rocks on his seat back and forth*). Hold on . . . How do you mean that. What for?

WASSILISSA. Free me from my husband. Take that halter from my neck . . .

PEPEL (*whistles*). Oho, I se-e! You have thought it out well . . . the husband in his grave, the admirer in Siberia, and you yourself . . .

WASSILISSA. But Waska, why Siberia? Not you yourself . . . your comrades. And even if you did do it yourself—who would know? Think . . . Natasha . . . thine . . . You shall have money . . . to go away . . . anywhere . . . you free me forever . . . and for my sister too; it will be a good thing for her to be away from me. I can't look at her without getting furious . . . I hate her on your account . . . I cannot control myself . . . I give her such blows that I myself cry for pity . . . but—I strike her just the same. And I will go on with it.

PEPEL. Beast! Don't sing praises of your own cruelty.

WASSILISSA. I am not praising myself. I only speak the truth. Remember, Waska, you have already been imprisoned twice by my husband . . . when you could not satisfy his greed . . . He sticks to me like vermin . . . for four years he has fed on me. Such a man for a husband!

And Natasha dreads him too. He oppresses her and calls her a beggar. He is a poison, a rank poison for us all . . .

PEPEL. How cleverly you contrive it all . . .

WASSILISSA. What I have said is not contrived . . . It is quite clear to you . . . Only a fool could not comprehend . . . (KOSTILIOFF *enters warily, L. U. E., and sneaks forward.*)

PEPEL (*to* WASSILISSA). No . . . go away!

WASSILISSA. Think it over. (*Sees her husband.*) What's this! Dogging me again? (PEPEL *springs up and looks wildly at* KOSTILIOFF.)

KOSTILIOFF. Indeed . . . it is I . . . it is I . . . and you are quite alone here? Ah . . . ah . . . Been chatting for a spell? (*Suddenly stamps his feet and screeches aloud, to* WASSILISSA.) Waska, you baggage . . . you beggar, you deceptive carrion. (*Then frightened by his own cry which is answered only by an echoless silence.*) Have mercy on me, Lord . . . You have again led me to sin, Wassilissa . . . I search for you everywhere . . . (*squeakingly*). It is time to go to bed. Have you forgot to fill the holy lamp? . . . ah, you beggar, you swine! (*Waves his hands tremblingly in her face.* WASSILISSA *goes slowly to the door, L. U. E., and looks back at* PEPEL.)

PEPEL (*to* KOSTILIOFF). You! Go your own way. Get out . . .

KOSTILIOFF (*cries*). I am the master here: Get out yourself, understand? Thief!

PEPEL (*sternly*). Go your own way, Mishka . . .

KOSTILIOFF. Be careful! Or else I'll . . . (PEPEL *seizes him by the collar and shakes him. A noise of turning and yawning is heard on the stove.* PEPEL *loosens* KOSTILIOFF, *who, crying loudly, goes out R. U. E. up the stairs.*)

PEPEL (*jumps on pritsche before stove*). Who is there? Who is on the stove?

LUKA (*poking his head out*). What?

PEPEL. Is it you?

LUKA (*composedly*). I . . . I myself . . . of Lord Jesus! Who else would it be.

PEPEL (*closes door L. U. E., looks for key, but does not find it*). The devil . . . crawl down, pilgrim.

LUKA. All right . . . I'll crawl down . . .

PEPEL (*roughly*). Why did you climb up on the stove?

LUKA. Where should I go?

PEPEL. Why didn't you go out into the entry?

LUKA. Too cold, little brother . . . I am an old man . . .

PEPEL. Did you hear?

LUKA. Without any trouble? Why not? I am not deaf. Ah, my boy, you are lucky, truly lucky.

PEPEL (*mistrustfully*). I am lucky? How so?

LUKA. Because . . . I climbed up on the stove . . . that was your luck . . .

PEPEL. Why did you move about?

LUKA. Because I feel hot . . . luckily for you, my orphan . . . and then I thought: if the boy does not lose his head . . . and strangle the old man . . .

PEPEL. Yes, I might easily have done it . . . I hate him . . .

LUKA. It would not have been any wonder . . . such things happen every day.

PEPEL (*laughing*). Hm . . . Have you yourself not done something of the kind some time?

LUKA. Listen, my boy, to what I tell you: this woman, keep well away from her. At no cost let her approach . . .

She will soon get her husband out of the way. Cleverer than you could ever manage it. Don't listen to her, off-spring of Satan! Look at me: not a hair left on my head . . . and why? The women, and no other reason . . . I have known, perhaps, more women than I have had hairs on my head . . . and this Wassilissa . . . is worse than the pest . . .

PEPEL. I don't know . . . whether to thank you . . . or, are you too . . .

LUKA. Say no more . . . Listen. If there is a girl, take the one you like best—take her by the hand and go away together; quite away, a long way off . . .

PEPEL (*gloomily*). We cannot know each other: who is good, who is bad . . . Nothing . . . is comprehensible.

LUKA. Of what importance can that be? Man's ways vary . . . following the different desires of his heart; so he lives, good today, bad tomorrow. And you love the girl, then pull out, settle it . . . Or go alone. You are young, you have still time enough ahead to . . . enmeshed by a woman.

PEPEL (*takes him by the shoulder*). No, but say—why do you tell me all this . . .

LUKA. Hold on. Let me go . . . I must look after Anna . . . Her throat is rattling. (*He goes to* ANNA'S *bed, strikes the curtain back, looks at the prostrate form and touches it with his hand.* PEPEL, *uneasy and depressed, follows him.*) Lord Jesus Christ, All Powerful! receive in peace the soul of this newcomer, thy servant Anna . . .

PEPEL (*whispers*). Is she dead? (*Elevates himself to his full height and looks without approaching.*)

LUKA (*whispering*). Her misery is ended. And where is her husband?

PEPEL. In the barroom—of course.

LUKA. He must be told . . .

PEPEL (*shrinking*). I do not love the dead.

LUKA (*goes to the door, L. U. E.*). Why should we love the dead? We must love the living . . . the living . . .

PEPEL. I'll go with you.

LUKA. Are you afraid?

PEPEL. I love them not . . . (*Ex. hastily, with* LUKA, *L. U. E. The stage remains empty for a few moments. Behind the door, L. U. E., is heard a dull, confused, unusual sound. Enter the* ACTOR, *L. U. E. He remains standing on the platform, his hand on the door jamb, and cries.*)

ACTOR. Old Man! Luka! Heh, where do you hide? Now I remember. Listen. (*Tremblingly takes two steps forward, puts himself in an attitude and declaims.*)

> And if humanity to holy truth,
>     No path by searching finds,
> Then all the world shall praise the fool,
>     Who spins a dream to mesh their minds.

(NATASHA *appears behind the* ACTOR *in the door. He continues.*) Old man . . . listen!

> And if the sun tomorrow shall forget
>     Upon the earth his light to stream,
> Then all the world shall hail the fool,
>     With his illuminating red-gold dream.

NATASHA (*laughs*). Look at the scarecrow. Maybe he has had one or two . . .

ACTOR (*turns to her*). A-ah, it is you! And where is

our patriarch? Our loving, kind-hearted pilgrim . . .
There is nobody . . . at home . . . Natasha, farewell,
farewell.

NATASHA (*approaches him*). You have just greeted
me, and now you say farewell.

ACTOR (*steps in her way*). I shall go . . . I shall travel
. . . when, soon as spring comes, I shall be far away.

NATASHA. Let me by . . . Where shall you travel
then?

ACTOR. I shall go to that city . . . I shall be cured
. . . You must leave here, too . . . Ophelia . . . get thee
to a nunnery . . . There is, you know, a hospital for
organisms . . . for hard drinkers, so to speak . . . a
splendid hospital . . . all marble . . . marble floors . . .
light . . . cleanliness . . . good board—all free of charge!
And marble floors, truly. I shall find it, this city, I'll be
myself again . . . Begin a new life . . . I am on the way
to regeneration . . . as King Lear said! Do you know
too, Natasha . . . what my stage name is? Svertchkoff-
Savolszhinski I'm called . . . nobody knows that here,
nobody . . . here I am nameless . . . realize, if you can
how it hurts to lose your name? Even dogs have their
names. (NATASHA *goes softly around the* ACTOR, *stands at*
ANNA's *bed and looks at the dead*.) Without a name . . .
where there is no name there is no man.

NATASHA. Look! . . . dear . . . why . . . she is dead . . .

ACTOR (*shaking his head*). Impossible . . .

NATASHA (*stands aside*). In God's name . . . look . . .

BUBNOFF (*enters L. U. E.*). What is there to look at?

NATASHA. Anna is dead!

BUBNOFF. Then there will be no more coughing. (*Goes*

*to* ANNA's *bed, looks for a time at the dead, and then goes to his place.)*   Somebody must tell Kleshtsch . . . it's his business . . .

ACTOR.   I'll go. I shall tell him . . . She too, has lost her name.

NATASHA (*Ex.* ACTOR *L. U. E. In the center of the room, to herself partly).*   And I . . . some time, shall languish so, and die forsaken in a cellar . . .

BUBNOFF (*spreading out an old torn blanket on his shelf).*   What is the matter . . . what are you muttering?

NATASHA.   Nothing . . . only to myself . . .

BUBNOFF.   Are you expecting Waska? Be careful with Waska . . . He will knock your skull in, some day, for you . . .

NATASHA.   Isn't it all the same to me, who knocks it in? I'd rather have it done by him . . .

BUBNOFF (*lies down).*   As you prefer . . . no funeral of mine.

NATASHA.   It is the best thing for her that could happen . . . to die . . . yet it is pitiful . . . thou loving Master . . . what did she live for?

BUBNOFF.   So with everybody—but, we live. Man is born, lives for a space of time, and dies. I will die too . . . and you will die . . . why pity the dead, then? (LUKA, *the* TARTAR, KRIVOI ZOBA *and* KLESHTSCH *enter L. U. E.* KLESHTSCH *follows behind the others in shaking spirits.)*

NATASHA.   Sh-sh . . . Anna!

KRIVOI ZOBA.   We have already heard . . . God take her soul . . .

TARTAR (*to* KLESHTSCH).   She must be taken out. She must be carried into the entry. This is no place for the dead. The living person can have a bed . . .

KLESHTSCH (*whispering*). We will take her out . . .
(*All stand around the body.* KLESHTSCH *looks at the remains of his wife over the shoulders of the others*).

KRIVOI ZOBA (*to the* TARTAR). Do you think she will smell? No . . . while she was still alive she dried up . . .

NATASHA. For God's sake . . . nobody pities her . . . if anybody had but said a word of kindness.

LUKA. Don't be hurt, my daughter. It is nothing. What have we to do with pitying the dead? We have not enough even for each other. And you talk of pitying her.

BUBNOFF (*gapes*). Why waste words . . . when she is dead—no words can help her any more . . . against sickness certain words can be used . . . against death, nothing.

TARTAR (*stepping aside*). The police must be told . . .

KRIVOI ZOBA. Naturally—that is the regulation. Kleshtsch, have you already reported it?

KLESHTSCH. No . . . now comes the funeral and I have only forty copecs in the world . . .

KRIVOI ZOBA. Then borrow . . . or we will take up a collection . . . everybody give what he can, one five copecs, another ten . . . but the police must soon be told. Or else, at last, they will think you have beaten your wife to death . . . or something else. (*Goes to the bunk, U. on which the* TARTAR *is lying, and attempts to lie down with him.*)

NATASHA (*goes to* BUBNOFF's *bench*). Now I shall dream about her . . . I always dream of the dead . . . I am afraid to be alone . . . It is so dark in the entry.

LUKA (*follows with his eyes*). Be afraid of the living . . . that I say to you . . .

NATASHA.   Take me up-stairs, daddy . . .

LUKA.   Come . . . come . . . I will go with you. (*Ex. both L. U. E. Pause.*)

KRIVOI ZOBA (*yawns*).   Oh, Oh! (*To the* TARTAR.)   It will soon be spring now, Hassan . . . Then there will be a little bit of sun for you and me. The peasants now are repairing their plows and harrows . . . they will go to the field soon . . . hm—yes . . . and we, Hassan. He is already snoring, cursed Mohammedan.

BUBNOFF.   The Tartars are fond of sleep.

KLESHTSCH (*standing in the middle of the room staring stupidly before himself*).   What shall I begin to do now?

KRIVOI ZOBA.   Lie down and sleep . . . that's all . . .

KLESHTSCH (*whispers*).   And . . . she! What shall be done with her? (*Nobody answers him. Enter* SAHTIN *and the* ACTOR, *L. U. E.*)

ACTOR (*cries*).   Old Man! My true adviser . . .

SAHTIN.   Miklucka-Maclai comes . . . ho, ho!

ACTOR.   The thing is settled! Patriarch, where is the city . . . where are you?

SAHTIN.   Fata Morgana! He has deluded you . . . there are no cities . . . No, no people . . . there is nothing at all!

ACTOR.   Liar . . .

TARTAR (*springing up*).   Where is the proprietor? I'll see the proprietor! If we can't sleep here, he shall charge us nothing . . . the dead . . . the drunken . . . (*Ex. quickly, R. U. E.* SAHTIN *whistles after him.*)

BUBNOFF (*awakened*).   Go to bed, brats, make no noise, the night is for sleep . . .

ACTOR.   True . . . I have here (*rubs his forehead*).

'Our nets have caught the dead,' as it says in a . . . chanson, from Beranger.*

SAHTIN. The dead hear not. The dead feel not. Howl . . . shout as much as you like . . . the dead hear not! (LUKA *appears in the door.*)

* In reality a quotation from Pushkin.

# ACT III*

*A vacant place between two buildings, filled with rubbish and overgrown with weeds. In the background, a high brick fire-wall, which covers the heavens. Near it a small elder-tree. On the right, a dark wall of reinforced wooden beams, part of a bar or stable. On the left, the gray wall of* KOSTILIOFF'*s lodging-house, its rough plaster adhering only in places. This wall runs diagonally, the rear wall of the building, the corner being about the middle of the scene, forming with the fire-wall a narrow passageway. In the gray wall there are two windows, one on a level with the earth, the other four or five feet higher and nearer the rear. Against the gray wall lies a great sled, overturned, with a tongue perhaps three yards long. Near the stable wall on the right is a heap of old boards and hewn beams.*

*It is evening, the setting sun throws a red light against the firewall. Spring has just begun and the snow is scarcely melted. The black twigs of the elder-tree have not begun to swell.*

*On the sled-tongue, side by side sit* NATASHA *and* NASTIAH. *On the pile of board* LUKA *and the* BARON.

* TRANSLATOR'S NOTE: In the Russian, the third act takes place upon a new scene, but as the scene of the previous acts may be employed without necessitating any change in dialogue or construction, the stage directions given in this act have the old scene in view. The new scene is described as follows:

62

KLESHTSCH *lies on a heap of wood near the right wall.*
BUBNOFF *is looking out of the lower window.*

NASTIAH (*with closed eyes, moving her head in time
to the story, which she is telling in a sing song voice*).
In the night, then, he came to the garden, to the summer-
bower, as we had arranged . . . I had waited long, trembling for fear and grief . . . and he too, was trembling
from head to foot, and chalk white, but in his hand he held
a . . . pistol . . .

NATASHA (*nibbling at sunflower seeds*).   Just listen
. . . these students are all as mad as March hares.

NASTIAH.   And in a terrible voice, he said to me: my
true love . . .

BUBNOFF.   Ha, ha, my 'true' love, did he say?

BARON.   Be still there, let her humbug in peace—you
don't have to listen, if it don't please you . . . go on.

NASTIAH.   My heart's distraction, said he, my golden
treasure; my parents refuse to allow me, said he, to marry
you, and threaten me with their curses if I do not give you
up, and so I must, said he, take my life . . . and his pistol
was frightfully large, and loaded with ten bullets . . .
Farewell, said he, true friend of my heart! My decision is
irrevocable . . . I cannot live without you. But I answered
him, my never-to-be-forgotten friend . . . my Raoul . . .

BUBNOFF (*astonished*).   What's his name . . . Graul?

BARON.   You are mistaken, Nastya! The last time you
called him Gaston.

NASTIAH (*springing up*).   Silence! You vagabond curs!
Can you understand what love is . . . real, genuine love!
And I . . . I have tasted this genuine love (*to the* BARON).
You unworthy scamp . . . You were an educated man
. . . you say, have drunk your coffee in bed . . .

LUKA. Have patience! Don't scold her! Show human beings some consideration . . . It is not what man says but why he says it—that's the point. Keep on, my love— They don't mean anything.

BUBNOFF. Always laying on the bright hues, raven . . . Nyah, cut loose again!

BARON. Go on.

NATASHA. Pay no attention to them . . . who are they, any way? They only speak out of envy . . . because they have nothing to tell about themselves . . .

NASTIAH (*sits down again*). I don't want . . . I won't tell anything more . . . if they don't like to believe it . . . and laugh about it. (*Suddenly brightens up. Is silent a few seconds, closes her eyes again and begins in a loud and rapid voice, keeping time with her hand, while in the distance ringing music is heard.*) And I answered him: Joy of my life! You my glittering star! Without you I too could not live . . . because I love you madly and must love you always, as long as my heart beats in my bosom! But, said I, rob yourself not of your young life . . . for look, your dear parents whose single you you are—they stand in need of you. Give me up . . . I would rather pine away . . . out of longing for you, my love . . . I am —alone . . . I am—wholly yours . . . yes, let me die . . . what matters it . . . I am good for nothing . . . and have nothing . . . absolutely nothing . . . (*covers her face with her hands and cries softly.*)

NATASHA (*goes to her side, quickly*). Don't. (LUKA *strokes* NASTIAH'S *head, laughing.*)

BUBNOFF (*laughs aloud*). Oh . . . ho . . . a deceiving minx, . . . eh?

BARON (*laughs aloud*). Now—Grandfather—do you

believe what she tells? She gets it all out of her book . . . out of "Disastrous Love," all nonsense. Drop it.

NATASHA. What is that to you? Keep still, rather. God has punished you enough . . .

NASTIAH (*furious*). You! Tell us, where is your soul!

LUKA (*takes her by the hand*). Come, my love. Do not be angry . . . They mean nothing, I know . . . I—believe you. You are right, and not they . . . if you yourself believe it, then you have had just such true love . . . Certainly, quite certainly. And he there, thy . . . lover, don't be angry . . . He only laughs perhaps . . . about it . . . because he is envious . . . No doubt in his whole life he never felt anything genuine . . . No, certainly not. Come!

NASTIAH (*presses her arm against her breast*). Grandfather. Before God . . . it is true! It is all true . . . A French student . . . Gastoscha was his name . . . and he had a little black beard . . . he always wore patent leather shoes . . . May lightning strike me instantly if it isn't true! And how he loved me . . . oh, how he loved me.

LUKA. I am sure. Say no more. I believe you. He wore patent leather shoes, you say? Aye, aye, and you have naturally loved him too. (*Ex. both L. U. E.*)

BARON. A stupid thing, good hearted but stupid, intolerably stupid.

BUBNOFF. How can a man lie so unceasingly? As if before a coroner.

NATASHA. Falsehood must indeed be pleasanter than the truth . . . I . . . too.

BARON. What 'I too?' Say more.

NATASHA. I too think of lots of them . . . to myself . . . and wait . . .

BARON. For what?

NATASHA (*laughing embarassed*). So . . . perhaps, think I . . . somebody will come tomorrow . . . some strange person . . . or there may happen . . . something that never happened before . . . I have already waited long . . . I still am waiting . . . and after all . . . to look at it right . . . can anything great be expected? (*Pause.*)

BARON (*laughing*). We can expect nothing at all . . . I least of all—I expect nothing more. For me everything has already been. All is past . . . at an end . . . what more?

NATASHA. Sometimes, too, I imagine, that tomorrow . . . I will die suddenly . . . which fills me with fear . . . In summer we think unwillingly of death . . . then comes the storm, and every moment one may be struck by lightning . . .

BARON. Your life has not been laid in easy lines . . . Your sister has the disposition of a fiend.

NATASHA. Whose life is easy? All have it hard, as far as I can see . . .

KLESHTSCH (*who has previously lain silent and motionless, springing up*). All? That is not true! Not all! If it was hard for all . . . then each of us could stand it . . . there would be nothing to complain about.

BUBNOFF. Say, are you possessed by the devil? Why howl? (KLESHTSCH *lies down again and stares vacantly.*)

BARON. I must see what Nastya is doing . . . I'll have to make up with her . . . or we shall have no more money for whisky.

BUBNOFF. People can never stop lying! I can understand Nastyka; she is accustomed to painting her cheeks

. . . So she tries it with the soul . . . paints her little soul red . . . but the rest, why do they do it? Luka, for example . . . turns everything into stories . . . without ceremony . . . why does he always lie? . . . at his age? . . .

BARON (*goes L. U. E. laughing*). All of us have gray souls . . . We like to lay on a bit of red.

LUKA (*enters from L. U. E.*). Tell me, Baron, why do you torment the girl. Let her alone . . . Can't she cry to pass the time away . . . she only sheds tears for pleasure . . . what harm can that do you?

BARON. She is a soft-brained thing, pilgrim . . . It's hard to swallow . . . today Raoul, tomorrow Gaston . . . and everlastingly one and the same. But anyway, I'll make up with her again. (*Ex. L. U. E.*).

LUKA. Go, treat her with friendliness . . . treat every one with friendliness—injure no one.

NATASHA. How good you are, grandfather . . . how is it that you are so good?

LUKA. I am good, you say. Nyah . . . if it is true, all right . . . (*Behind the red wall is heard soft singing and accordion playing*). But you see, my girl—there must be some one to be good . . . We must have pity on mankind. Christ, remember, has pity for us all and so taught us to be so. Have pity when there is still time, believe me, it is very good. I was once, for example, employed as a watchman, at a country place which belonged to an engineer, not far from the city of Tomsk, in Siberia. The house stood in the middle of the forest, an out-of-the-way location . . . and it was winter and I was all alone in the country house . . . It was beautiful there . . . magnificent! And once . . . I heard them scrambling up!

NATASHA. Thieves!

LUKA. Yes. They crept higher and I took my rifle and went outside. I looked up: two men . . . as they were opening a window and so busy that they did not see anything of me at all . . . I cried to them: hey there . . . get out of that . . . and would you think it, they fell on me with a hand ax . . . I warned them—Halt, I cried, or else I fire . . . then I aimed first at one and then at the other. They fell on their knees saying, pardon us. I was pretty hot . . . on account of the hand ax, you remember. You devils, I cried, I told you to clear out and you didn't . . . and now, I said, one of you go into the brush and get a switch. It was done: and now, I commanded, one of you stretch out on the ground, and the other thrash him . . . and so they whipped each other at my command. And when they had each had a sound beating, they said to me: grandfather, said they, for the sake of Christ give us a piece of bread. We haven't a bite in our bodies. They, my daughter, were the thieves, (*laughs*) who had fallen upon me with the hand ax. Yes . . . they were a pair of splendid fellows . . . I said to them, if you had asked for bread. Then they answered: we had gotten past that . . . we had asked and asked and nobody would give us anything . . . endurance was worn out . . . nyah, and so they remained with me the whole winter. One of them, Stephen by name, liked to take the rifle and go into the woods . . . and the other, Jakoff, was constantly ill, always coughing . . . the three of us watched the place, and when spring came, they said, farewell, grandfather, and went away—to Russia . . .

NATASHA. Were they convicts, escaping?

LUKA. They were . . . fugitives . . . they had left

their colony . . . a pair of splendid fellows . . . If I had not had pity on them . . . who knows what would have happened. They might have killed me . . . Then they would be taken to court again, put in prison, sent back to Siberia . . . why all that? You learn nothing good in prison, nor in Siberia . . . but a man, what can he not learn. Man may teach his fellowman something good . . . very simply. (*Pause.*)

BUBNOFF. Hm . . . yes . . . and I . . . can never lie. Why should I do it? Always out with the truth, that is my way of thinking, whether it pleases or not. Why trouble to be considerate?

KLESHTSCH (*springing up, as though stabbed, crying*). What is the truth? Where is the truth—where! (*Beats with his hands on his torn clothes.*) There is the truth— there! No work . . . No strength . . . in the limbs—that is the truth! No shelter . . . no shelter . . . It is time to die, that is your truth, curse it! What is it to me, this— truth? Only let me sigh in peace—let me sigh. What have I done? Why should we have truth, to the devil? Curse it, we can't live . . . that is the truth!

BUBNOFF. Listen though . . . he is full of matter . . .

LUKA. The good Lord . . . but say, my friend, thou . . .

KLESHTSCH (*trembling with excitement*). I have heard you talk of the truth. You, pilgrim—you consoling every one . . . and I say to you: I hate everyone. And this truth . . . Hast understood? Mark you, accursed shall truth be. (*Hurries out, L. U. E., looking back as he goes.*)

LUKA. Ay, ay, ay; but he is out of his head . . . and where can he be running?

NATASHA. He rages away like one gone mad.

BUBNOFF. He laid it all down in the proper order . . .

as in a theatre . . . the same thing happens often . . . he is not accustomed to life . . .

PEPEL (*enters slowly L. U. E.*). Peace to you honest folks! Nyah, Luka, old devil—telling more stories?

LUKA. You ought to have seen just now, a man crying out.

PEPEL. Kleshtsch, you mean, hm? What is the matter with him now? He ran past me, as if he were crazy . . .

LUKA. You will run the same way too, when once it gets into your heart . . .

PEPEL (*sits*). I can't endure him . . . he is embittered, and proud. (*He imitates* KLESHTSCH.) 'I am a working-man . . .' as though others were inferior to him . . . Work, indeed, if it gives you pleasure . . . but why do you need to be so proud about it? If you estimate men by work, then a horse is better than any man. He pulls a wagon—and holds his mouth about it. Natasha . . . are your people at home?

NATASHA. They have gone to the grave-yard . . . after a while, church . . .

PEPEL. You've therefore, leisure . . . that happens seldom.

LUKA (*thoughtfully to* BUBNOFF). You say—the truth . . . but the truth is not a cure for every ill . . . you cannot always heal the soul with truth . . . for example, the following case: I knew a man who believed in the land of justice . . .

BUBNOFF. In wh-at?

LUKA. In the land of justice. There must be, said he, a land of justice somewhere in the world . . . in which un-usual men, so to speak, must live . . . good men, who respect each other, who help each other when they can . . .

everything there is good and beautiful. It is a country which every man should seek . . . He was poor and things went bad with him . . . so bad, indeed, that soon nothing remained for him to do but to lie down and die—but still he did not lose courage. He often laughed and said to himself: it makes no difference—I can bear it! Still a little while I'll wait—then throw this life aside and go into the land of justice . . . it was his only pleasure . . . this land of justice . . .

PEPEL. Yes, and . . . Has he gone there?

BUBNOFF. Where! Ha, ha, ha!

LUKA. At that time there was brought to the place—the thing happened in Siberia—an exile, a man of learning . . . with books and maps and all sorts of arts . . . And the sick man spoke to the sage: Tell me, I implore you, where lies the land of justice, and how can one succeed in getting there. Then the learned man opened his books and spread his maps out, and searched and searched, but he found the land of justice nowhere. Everything else was correct, all countries were shown—the land of justice alone did not appear.

PEPEL (softly). No? Was it really not there? (BUBNOFF laughs).

NATASHA. What are you laughing at? Go on, grandfather.

LUKA. The man would not believe him . . . It must be there, said he . . . look more closely! For all your books and maps, said he, are not worth a whistle if the land of justice is not shown on them. The learned man felt himself insulted. My maps, said he, are absolutely correct, and a land of justice nowhere exists. So, the other was furious. What, he cried—have I now lived and lived and lived, endured and endured, and always believed there was such a country. And according to your plans there is none! That is robbery . . . and he said to the learned man: you good-for-nothing scamp . . . you are a cheat and no sage. Then he gave him a sound blow over the skull, and still another . . . (*is silent a few moments*). And then he went home and choked himself . . . (*all are silent.* LUKA *looks silently at* PEPEL *and* NATASHA.)

PEPEL.   The devil take him . . . the story is not cheerful . . .

NATASHA.   He couldn't stand it . . . to be so disappointed.

BUBNOFF (*in a surly tone*).   All tales . . .

PEPEL.   Hm, yes . . . there is your land of justice . . . it was not to be found it appears . . .

NATASHA.   One should have sympathy for him . . . the poor man . . .

BUBNOFF.   All imagination . . . ha, ha! The land of justice—stuff! Ha, ha, ha, ha! (*exit in kitchen.*)

LUKA (*looking after him*).   He laughs, ah, yes. children . . . farewell . . . I shall leave you soon . . .

PEPEL.   Where do you journey, then?

LUKA.   To Little Russia . . . I hear they have discovered a new religion there . . . I will see what it is . . . yes . . . Man searches and searches, always looking for something better . . . may God give them patience.

PEPEL.   Think you, they will find it?

LUKA.   Who? Mankind? Certainly they shall find it . . . He who yearns . . . he finds . . . who searches zealously—he finds!

NATASHA.   I wish them a happy journey. I hope they will find something.

LUKA. That shall they surely do. But we must help them, my daughter . . . must respect them . . .

NATASHA. How shall I help them? I am myself . . . so helpless . . .

PEPEL (*restrained*). Listen to me, Natasha . . . I want to speak to you . . . in his presence . . . he knows it . . . come . . . with me!

NATASHA. Where? To prisons?

PEPEL. I have already told you that I will give up stealing. By God, I will! When I say a thing, I keep my word. I have learned to read and write . . . I can easily make a living. (*With a movement of the hand towards* LUKA.) He advised me—to try it in Siberia . . . to go of my own accord . . . How does it strike you—shall we go? Believe me, I am sick of this life. Ah, Natasha! I see indeed how things are . . . I have consoled my conscience with the thought that others steal more than I—and are still respected . . . but how does that help me . . . not in the least. But I have no regret . . . nor do I believe, any conscience . . . But I feel one thing: that I must live in a different way. I must live better . . . I must live . . . so that I can respect myself . . .

LUKA. Quite right, my boy. May God be with you . . . May Christ help you! Well resolved: a man must respect himself . . .

PEPEL. From childhood, I have been—only a thief . . . Always I was called, Waska, the pickpocket, Waska, the son of a thief! See, it was of no consequence to me, as long as they would have it so . . . so they would have it . . . I was a thief, perhaps, only out of spite . . . because nobody came along to call me anything except—thief . . . You call me something else, Natasha . . . now?

NATASHA (*in low spirits*). I do not quite believe it all . . . words and words . . . and then . . . I don't know . . . Today I am disquieted . . . my heart is despondent . . . As though I dreaded something. You would not begin today, Wassili . . .

PEPEL. What else, then! This is not the first time I have spoken . . .

NATASHA. Shall I go with you . . . I love you . . . not too much . . . Sometimes I like you . . . but then at times I cannot look at you . . . in any case I do not love . . . when one loves, one sees no fault in the beloved . . . and I see faults in you . . .

PEPEL. You will soon love me, have no fear! You will become accustomed to me . . . only say 'yes.' For over a year I have been watching you, and I see that you are an honest girl . . . a good, true woman . . . I love you with all my heart. (WASSILISSA, *still in gay street dress, appears at the door at the head of the stair, R. U. E. She stands with one hand on the balustrade and the other on the door post and laughs.*)

NATASHA. So . . . you love me with all your heart, and my sister . . .

PEPEL (*embarrassed*). What do I care for her? Her kind is nothing . . .

LUKA. It does not matter, my daughter. One eats turnips when he has no bread . . .

PEPEL (*gloomily*). Have pity on me. It is no easy life that I lead—friendless; pursued like a wolf . . . I sink like a man in a swamp . . . whatever I clutch is slimy and rotten . . . nothing is firm . . . your sister, though, would be different . . . if she were not so avaricious . . . I would have risked everything for her . . . If she had only kept faith with me . . . but her heart is for something else . . . her heart is full of greed . . . and longs for freedom . . . and only that longing in order to become more dissolute. She cannot help me . . . but you—like a young fir-tree, you are prickly but you give support . . .

LUKA.   And I say to you: take him, my daughter, take him. He is a good-hearted boy. All you must do is to remind him often, that he is good . . . so that he will not forget it. He will soon believe you. Only say to him, often, Waska, you are a good man . . . don't forget it! Think it over, my love—what else shall you begin? Your sister—she is a bad lot: and of her husband—nothing good can be said either: no words can be found to express his baseness . . . and this whole life here . . . where shall you find a way out? . . . But Waska . . . he is a lusty fellow.

NATASHA.   I cannot find a way . . . I know that . . . I have already thought it over myself . . . but I . . . who can I trust . . . I see no way out . . .

PEPEL.   There is but one way . . . but I shall not let you take it . . . I would kill you first . . .

NATASHA (*laughing*).   Just look . . . I am not yet your wife, and you will already kill me.

PEPEL (*putting his arms around her*).   Say 'yes,' Natasha. It will soon be well . . .

NATASHA (*pressing him affectionately*)   . . . One thing I will tell you, Wassili . . . And God shall be my witness: if you strike me a single time . . . or insult me . . . that shall be the end . . . either I hang myself, or . . .

PEPEL.   My hand shall wither up, if I touch you . . .

LUKA.   Don't be troubled, my love, you can believe him. You are necessary to his happiness, and he to yours . . .

WASSILISSA (*from above*). And the match is made. May God give you love and harmony.

NATASHA. They are already back . . . Oh, God! They have seen us . . . ah, Wassili!

PEPEL. What are you afraid of? Nobody dares touch you now!

WASSILISSA. Do not be afraid, Natalya. He will not strike you . . . He can neither strike, nor love . . . I know him.

LUKA (*softly*). Ah, such a woman . . . a venomous snake . . .

WASSILISSA. He is only bold with words . . .

KOSTILIOFF (*enters R. from kitchen*). Nataschka! What are you doing here, lazy-bones? Gossiping, eh! Complaining about your relatives: the samovar is not in order, the table not cleared off!

NATASHA (*going R. kitchen*). You were going to church, I thought . . .

KOSTILIOFF. It does not concern you what we are going to do. Mind your own business . . . do what you are told.

PEPEL. Shut up. She is not your servant now . . . Natalya, don't budge . . . don't move a finger.

NATASHA. It is not for you to give orders here . . . Too soon yet for orders (*Ex. R.*)

PEPEL (*to* KOSTILIOFF). Enough of that. You have mortified the poor girl enough! She is mine now.

KOSTILIOFF. You-u? When did you buy her? What did you pay for her? (WASSILISSA *laughs aloud*.)

LUKA. Waska! Get out . . .

PEPEL. Are you having a good time over me? You may weep yet!

WASSILISSA. What do you say! I am afraid of you. (*Laughs.*)

LUKA. Go away, Wassili! Don't you see how she plays with you . . . pricks you on—can't you understand?

PEPEL. Ah . . . so! (*To* WASSILISSA). Don't give yourself any trouble. What you want will not be done.

WASSILISSA. And what I do not want done, will not be done, Waska!

PEPEL (*threatens her with his fist*). We shall see . . . (*Ex. L. U. E.*).

WASSILISSA (*as she goes out R. U. E.*). I will prepare a glorious wedding for you.

KOSTILIOFF (*advances on* LUKA). So . . . .What are you stirring up, old man?

LUKA. Nothing, old man.

KOSTILIOFF. Um! You are going to leave us, I hear!

LUKA. It is time.

KOSTILIOFF. Where to?

LUKA. Wherever my nose points.

KOSTILIOFF. You are going to become a vagabond again. You seem to be a rolling stone . . .

LUKA. Resting iron is rusting iron, says the proverb.

KOSTILIOFF. That may be true of iron, but a man must remain in one place . . . Men cannot be tumbling about like cockroaches in the kitchen . . . first here, then there . . . A man must have a place which he can call home . . . He must not be crawling aimlessly about the earth.

LUKA. And if one—is at home everywhere?

KOSTILIOFF. Then he is only—a tramp . . . a good-for-nothing fellow . . . a man must make himself useful . . . he must work . . .

LUKA. What do you say?

KOSTILIOFF. Indeed! What else then? . . . You call yourself a wanderer, a pilgrim . . . What is a pilgrim? A pilgrim is one who goes his own way—keeps to himself . . . has peculiarities, so to speak, is unlike other people . . . that's understood about a true pilgrim . . . He ponders and unravels . . . and at last discovers something . . . perhaps the truth, who knows . . . He holds his truth for himself, and remains silent. If he is a true pilgrim, he remains silent . . . Or, he speaks so that no one understands him . . . He has no wish to be gratified, doesn't turn people's heads, does not butt-in. How others live— give him no concern . . . He lives proudly and in rectitude . . . searches out the forest and the unfrequented places . . . where no one comes. He is in nobody's way, condemns nobody . . . but prays for all . . . for all the sinners of this world . . . for me, for you . . . for all! He flies from the vanity of this world—to prayer. So it is. (*Pause.*) And you . . . what sort of a pilgrim are you . . . you have not even a passport . . . Every law abiding citizen must have a passport . . . all orderly people have passports . . . yes . . .

LUKA. There are people and there are men . . .

KOSTILIOFF. Don't get funny! Don't give us any riddles . . . I am not your fool . . . What do you mean by people—and men?

LUKA. Where is any riddle? I mean—there are stony fields which are not worth sowing . . . and there are fertile fields . . . whatever is sown thereon—yields a harvest . . . so it is . . .

KOSTILIOFF. And what does all this mean?

LUKA. You for example . . . If God himself said to you: 'Michailo, be a man,' it is certain that it would be useless . . . As you are, so you will remain for all times . . .

KOSTILIOFF. Ah . . . and do you know that my wife's uncle is on the police force? And if I . . .

WASSILISSA (*enters R.*). Michailo Ivanitsch, come drink your tea . . .

KOSTILIOFF (*to* LUKA). Hear me, you—keep out of this row—leave my house . . .

WASSILISSA. Yes, put on your knapsack, old man . . . your tongue is too long . . . who knows . . . perhaps you may be an escaped convict.

KOSTILIOFF. Be sure that you disappear today . . . or else . . . we shall see.

LUKA. Or else you will call your uncle, eh? Call him . . . tell him, you can catch a convict here, uncle . . . then your uncle will receive a reward . . . three copecs . . .

BUBNOFF (*looking out from over the stove*). What business are you haggling about . . . what is it . . . for three copecs . . . ?

LUKA. We are trying to see me.

WASSILISSA (*to her husband*). Let's go.

BUBNOFF. For three copecs. Take care old man . . . or they will sell you for one copec . . .

KOSTILIOFF (*to* BUBNOFF). What are you staring out of there for: like a hobgoblin out of a tunnel. (*Approaches R. with* WASSILISSA.)

WASSILISSA. How many blackbirds there are in the world . . . how many knaves.

LUKA. I wish you a good appetite.

WASSILISSA (*turns to him*). Take good care of yourself —you dirty frog stool. (*Ex. with* KOSTILIOFF *R.*)

LUKA. Tonight—I leave.

BUBNOFF. You'll do right. It is always best to go before it is too late . . .

LUKA. Quite right.

BUBNOFF. I speak from experience. I took my own departure once at the right moment, and saved myself a trip to Siberia.

LUKA. What do you say?

BUBNOFF. It is true. The case was thus: my wife had a love affair with my helper . . . and a very good helper he was, I must admit . . . he could make the most beautiful polar bear furs from dog skins . . . cat skins he dyed into kangaroos . . . into muskrats . . . into anything you could wish . . . a very clever fellow . . . My wife was madly in love with him. They hung on each other so much that I feared every moment they would poison me or put me out of the world in some other way. I whipped my wife often, and my helper whipped me . . . in a barbarous fashion he did the business too. Once he pulled half my beard out and broke a rib for me. Naturally I was not particular when I struck back . . . gave my wife one over the skull with an iron yard stick . . . we were generally fighting like good fellows . . . Finally I saw there was no chance for me . . . they would surely fix it for me. Then I arranged a plan—to kill my wife . . . I had quite made up my mind. But in the nick of time—I came to my senses —and cleared out of the row . . .

LUKA. It was better so, let them be quiet there making polar bears out of dogs.

BUBNOFF. Worse luck, the shop was in her name . . . only what I had on my back I kept . . . though, to speak

honestly, I would have drunk the place up in no time . . .
I am a glorious drunk, you understand.

LUKA. A glorious drunk.

BUBNOFF. Oh, a glorious drunk. When things come
my way I soak up everything in sight. And then I am
lazy . . . nothing is more terrible than work. (SAHTIN
*and the* ACTOR *come in quarrelling.*)

SAHTIN. Nonsense! You will go nowhere. You're talking stupid stuff. Tell me, pilgrim . . . what spark have
you been throwing into this burned stump?

ACTOR. You lie! Grandfather, tell him that he lies. I
go. I have worked today. I have cleaned the pavement
. . . and drunk no whisky. What do you say now? There,
see—two fifteeners, and I am sober.

SAHTIN. It is all wrong! Give it to me, I'll drink it
. . . or lose it at cards.

ACTOR. Let it alone. It is for the journey!

LUKA (*to* SAHTIN). Listen you—why do you try to
upset his resolution?

SAHTIN. 'Tell me, you wizard, darling of the gods—
what shall fate with my future do?' Moneyless, brother, I
have played everything away, broke. But the world is not
lost, old man, there are still sharper knaves than I.

LUKA. You are a lusty brother, Constantine . . . a
loveable man . . .

BUBNOFF. You actor, come here. (*The* ACTOR *goes to
the stove and talks apart with* BUBNOFF.)

SAHTIN. When I was still young, I was a jolly chicken.
I look back on it with pleasure . . . I had the soul of a
man . . . I danced splendidly, acted, was a famous bache-
lor . . . simply a phenomenal!

LUKA.   How then have you gotten so far afield . . . hm?

SAHTIN.   You are curious, old man. You would know all . . . and what for?

LUKA.   I always like to know about . . . mankind's difficulties . . . and I do not understand you, Constantine. When I look at you; such a loveable man . . . so sensible . . . then suddenly . . .

SAHTIN.   The prison, grandfather. Four years and seven months I have done, and coming out, a discharged convict, I found my course in life shut up . . .

LUKA.   Oh, oh, oh! Why then were you imprisoned?

SAHTIN.   On account of my own sister . . . Stop questioning . . . it annoys me . . . It is . . . an old story . . . my sister is dead . . . nine years have gone by . . . she was a splendid creature . . . my sister . . .

LUKA.   You take life easily. It falls more heavily on others . . . Do you just now, for example, hear the locksmith crying out—oh, oh!

SAHTIN.   Kleshtsch?

LUKA.   The same. No work, he cried . . . absolutely none . . .

SAHTIN.   You will get accustomed to that . . . Tell me, what shall I now begin to do?

LUKA (*softly*).   Look, there he comes . . . (KLESHTSCH *enters slowly L. U. E. with sunken head.*)

SAHTIN.   Heh, there, widower! What are you hanging your head about? What are you brooding over?

KLESHTSCH.   My skull is splitting from it . . . What shall I do now! My tools are gone . . . The funeral has eaten everything up . . .

SAHTIN.   I will give you a piece of advice. Do nothing

at all. Burden the earth with your weight—simple enough.

KLESHTSCH. You advise well . . . I—still am ashamed before others.

SAHTIN. Drop it . . . people are not ashamed to let you live worse than a dog. Just imagine if you would not work, and I would not work . . . and still hundreds and thousands of others would not work . . . and finally everybody—understand?—everybody quit work and nobody did anything at all—what, do you think, would happen then?

KLESHTSCH. Everybody would starve . . .

LUKA (to SAHTIN). There is such a sect. 'Jumpers,' they call themselves . . . They talk exactly like you . . .

SAHTIN. I know them . . . They are not at all such fools, pilgrim. (From KOSTILIOFF's room R. U. E. screaming.)

NATASHA (within). What are you doing—stop . . . what have I done?

LUKA (disquieted). Who is screaming there? Was it not Natasha? Ah, you . . . (From KOSTILIOFF's room is heard a loud alarm, and then from the kitchen the sound of crashing dishes.)

KOSTILIOFF (within, screaming). A—ah—you cat— you . . . heathen.

WASSILISSA (within). Wait . . . I'll give her . . . so . . . so . . . and so . . .

NATASHA (within). Help! They are killing me!

SAHTIN (runs up steps R. U. E. shouting). Heh, there! What are you howling about?

LUKA (walks about uneasily). Waska . . . he must be called . . . Wassili . . . Oh, God . . . Children, my dears.

ACTOR (*hurries out, L. U. E.*). I'll bring him . . . right away . . .

BUBNOFF. They are giving the poor girl bad treatment, quite often now.

SAHTIN. Come, pilgrim . . . We will be witnesses . . .

LUKA (*Exit after* SAHTIN *R.*). Why witnesses? Too often, already, have I been a witness. If Waska would only come . . . oh! trouble, trouble!

NATASHA (*within*). Sister . . . dear sister . . . wah . . . wa . . . a . . .

BUBNOFF. Now they have stopped her mouth . . . I'll see myself. (*The noise in* KOSTILIOFF's *room is weaker, and nothing comes from the kitchen.*)

KOSTILIOFF (*within*). Halt! (*A door is slammed within, and the whole noise is cut off as if by a hatchet. On the stage, silence. It is twilight.*)

KLESHTSCH (*sits on bench U. taking no part, and rubbing his hands together. Then he begins to mumble to himself, at first indistinctly. Then louder.*) How then? . . . a man must live . . . (*Louder.*) At least a shelter . . . but no, not that . . . not even a corner where I can lie down . . . Nothing but the bare man . . . helpless and deserted. (*Ex. bent over, L. U. E. slowly. For a few moments, ominous silence. Then somewhere within, on the R. a terrible noise, a chaos of tones, louder and louder and nearer and nearer. Then a single voice is heard.*)

WASSILISSA (*within*). I am her sister. Let me go . . .

KOSTILIOFF (*within*). What right have you to interfere?

WASSILISSA (*within*). You convict!

SAHTIN (*within*). Bring Waska . . . be quick . . . Zoba, strike (*a policemen's whistle is heard*).

TARTAR (*jumps down the steps, R. U. E., his right hand bound up*). What sort of laws are these . . . to murder in broad daylight. (KRIVOI ZOBA *hurries in L. U. E., followed by* KOSTILIOFF.)

KRIVOI ZOBA. Now, he got it from me.

MEDVIÉDEFF. How did you come to strike him?

TARTAR. And you—do you not know what your duty is?

MEDVIÉDEFF (*running after* KRIVOI ZOBA). Stop! Give me my whistle back. (*Ex. L. U. E.*)

KOSTILIOFF (*enters R. U. E.*). Abram! Catch him . . . hold him tight. He has killed me . . . (*Down the steps R. U. E. come* KVASCHNYA *and* NASTIAH. *They help* NAYASHA, *who is badly beaten up.* SAHTIN *runs up the stairs, bumping into* WASSILISSA, *who is throwing her arms about and trying to strike her sister.* ALYOSCHKA *is jumping around like one possessed. He whistles in* WASSILISSA'S *ear and howls. A couple of ragged fellows and some men and women appear L. U. E.*).

SAHTIN (*to* WASSILISSA). Where then, damned owl?

WASSILISSA. Away, convict. If it costs me my life, I will tear her to pieces.

KVASHNYA (*leads* NATASHA *aside*). Stop, Karpovna . . . have shame. How can you be so inhuman?

MEDVIÉDEFF (*re-enters L. U. E., takes* SAHTIN *by the collar*). Aha! Now I have you!

SAHTIN. Krivoi Zoba. Strike . . . Waska, Waska. (*All storm the entrance, L. U. E.* NATASHA *is taken to the bed, L.* PEPEL *enters L. U. E. Pushes them away.*) Where is Natasha, you?

KOSTILIOFF (*crouches on the steps R. U. E.*). Abram!

Catch Waska . . . brother, help catch Waska . . . the thief . . . the robber . . .

PEPEL. There, you old goat. (*Strikes* KOSTILIOFF *brutally.* PEPEL *hurries to* NATASHA.)

WASSILISSA. Fix Waska . . . friends . . . do up the thief!

MEDVIÉDEFF (*to* SAHTIN). You didn't have to mix in . . . this is a family affair here. They are all related to each other . . . and who are you?

PEPEL (*to* NATASHA). What did she hit you with? Did she stab you . . .

KVASCHNYA. Look what a beast. They have scalded her legs with hot water.

NASTIAH. They turned the samovar over . . .

TARTAR. It might have been an accident . . . if you are not sure you should not accuse . . .

NATASHA (*half unconscious*). Wassili . . . take me away . . . hide me . . .

WASSILISSA. Look, my friends . . . come here. He is dead . . . they have killed him . . . (*All gather at the landing.* BUBNOFF *separates himself from the others and crosses to* PEPEL.)

BUBNOFF (*softly*). Waska! The old man . . . is done for.

PEPEL (*looks at* BUBNOFF *as though he did not understand*). Get a cab . . . she must be taken to the hospital . . . I'll settle the bill.

BUBNOFF. Listen to what I'm saying. Somebody has finished the old man . . . (*The noise on the stage subsides like a fire into which water has been poured. Half aloud separate sentences are uttered*).

Is it really true?

We have it there.

Terrible.

We had better get out, brother.

The devil!

We need clear heads now.

Get out before the police come. (*The group becomes smaller.* BUBNOFF *and the* TARTAR *disappear.* NASTIAH *and* KVASCHNYA *stoop to* KOSTILIOFF'*s body.*)

WASSILISSA (*rises and cries in a triumphant tone*). They have killed him . . . my husband! And who did it? He, there! Waska killed him. Him. I saw it, my friends. I saw it! Now, Waska! Police! Police!

PEPEL (*leaves* NATASHA). Let me alone . . . get out of the way. (*Stares at the body. To* WASSILISSA.) Now? Now you are glad? (*Kicks the body*). Scotched at last . . . the old hound. Now you have your desire . . . Shall I treat you in the same way . . . and twist your neck. (*Falls on her, but is quietly caught by* SAHTIN *and* KRIVOI ZOBA. WASSILISSA *hides L. U. E.*)

SAHTIN. Come to your senses.

KRIVOI ZOBA. P-r-r-r! Where would you spring?

WASSILISSA (*appearing again*). Nyah, Waska, friend of my heart! Nobody escapes his fate . . . the police! Abram . . . whistle!

MEDVIÉDEFF. They have stolen my whistle, the fiends . . .

ALYOSCHKA. Here it is. (*He whistles,* MEDVIÉDEFF *chases him.*)

SAHTIN (*leads* PEPEL *back to* NATASHA). Don't worry, Waska. Killed in a row . . . a trifle! Only a short sentence for that . . .

WASSILISSA. Hold him tight. Waska murdered him . . . I saw it!

SAHTIN. I handed him a couple myself . . . How much does an old man need? Call me as a witness, Waska . . .

PEPEL. I . . . do I need to justify myself . . . But Wassilissa . . . I'll pull her into it! She wanted it done . . . She incited me to kill her husband . . . yes, she was the instigator . . .

NATASHA (*suddenly springing up*). Ah . . . (*In a loud voice*). Now it is clear . . . It stands so, Wassili! Listen, good people: it was all arranged. He and my sister, they plotted it out, they laid their plans! I see, Wassili! Before . . . you spoke with me . . . that was part of it! Good people, she is his mistress . . . you know it . . . everybody knows it . . . They understand each other. She, she instigated the murder . . . her husband was in the way . . . for that reason . . . she beat me so . . .

PEPEL. Natalija! What are you saying . . . What are you saying?

SAHTIN. Foolish chatter.

WASSILISSA. She lies! All of it is lies . . . I know of nothing . . . Waska killed him . . . he alone!

NATASHA. They have plotted it out . . . They shall be convicted . . . both of them . . .

SAHTIN. Here is a game for you . . . Now, Wassili, hold fast or they will drown you.

KRIVOI ZOBA. I can't understand . . . ah . . . far away from here.

PEPEL. Natalija. . . . Speak . . . are you in earnest? Can you believe that I . . . with her . . .

SAHTIN. For God's sake, Natasha, be sensible.

WASSILISSA (*on the landing*). They killed my husband . . . you high born . . . Waska Pepel, the thief killed him, Mr. Commissioner, I saw it . . . everybody saw it.

NATASHA (*waltzing about half senseless*). Good people . . . my sister and Waska . . . they killed him. Mr. Policeman . . . listen to me . . . these two, my sister put him up to it . . . her lover . . . she instigated him . . . there he is, the accursed—the two did it. Arrest them . . . take them to court . . . and take me, too . . . to prison with me! For the sake of God . . . to prison . . .

# ACT IV

*The same setting except that* PEPEL's *room is not to be seen, the partitions having been removed. The anvil, too, where* KLESHTSCH *sat, is gone. In the corner which was occupied by* PEPEL's *chamber is a pritsche on which the* TARTAR *lies, restlessly rolling about and groaning with pain.* KLESHTSCH *sits at the table repairing an accordion and now and then trying the chords. At the other end of the table sits* SAHTIN, *the* BARON, *and* NASTIAH. *Before them a bottle of spirits, three bottles of beer and a great hunk of black bread. On the stove the* ACTOR, *shifting about and coughing. It is night. The stage is lit by a lamp which is in the middle of the table. Outside the wind howls.*

KLESHTSCH. Y-es . . . In the midst of the row he disappeared.

BARON. He took flight before the police, as a fog before the sun.

SAHTIN. So all sinners fly before the face of the just.

NASTIAH. He was a splendid old man . . . and you are not men . . . you are rust . . .

BARON (*drinks*). To your health, lady!

SAHTIN. An interesting patriarch . . . truly! Our Nastiah fell in love with him.

NASTIAH. True . . . I fell in love with him. He had

an eye for everything . . . he understood everything . . .

SAHTIN (*laughs*). For some people he was a godsend . . . like mush for the toothless.

BARON (*laughs*). Or a poultice for an abscess.

KLESHTSCH. He had a sympathetic heart . . . you here . . . have no sympathy.

SAHTIN. What good would it do you for me to show you pity?

KLESHTSCH. You need not sympathize . . . but at least . . . do not injure me . . .

TARTAR (*gets up on his bench and moves his injured hand back and forth, as if it were a baby*). The old man was good . . . He had respect for the law in his heart . . . and whoever in his heart keeps the law . . . that man is good. He who does not—is lost . . .

BARON. What law do you mean, prince?

TARTAR. As you will . . . the law . . . the law to you . . . you understand me.

BARON. Go on.

TARTAR. Encroach upon no man . . . there you have the law . . .

SAHTIN. With us in Russia it is called, 'Code for Criminal Punishment and Correction.'

BARON. With another 'Code for Penalties Imposed by Justices of the Peace.'

TARTAR. With us it is called the Koran . . . Your Koran is your law . . . our Koran we must carry in our hearts.

KLESHTSCH (*tries the accordion*). Don't be forever hissing, beast. What the prince says is right . . . We must live according to the law . . . according to the gospels . . .

SAHTIN.   Live so.

BARON.   Try it.

TARTAR.   Mohammed gave us the Koran . . . there you have your law, he said. Do, as is written therein. Then a time shall come when the Koran will not suffice . . . a new time with new laws . . . for every epoch has its own laws . . .

SAHTIN.   Yes, of course, our epoch gives us 'Criminal Code.' A durable law, not so easily worn off.

NASTIAH (*knocks on the table with her knuckles*).   Now I would like to know . . . exactly why I live . . . here with you? I shall go . . . anywhere . . . to the end of the earth.

BARON.   Without shoes, lady?

NASTIAH.   Quite naked, as far as I care! I shall crawl on all fours if you please.

BARON.   That would be picturesque . . . on all fours . . .

NASTIAH.   I would do it . . . willingly . . . if I only need not have to look at your snout again . . . ah, how disgusting everything has become to me . . . my whole life . . . everybody.

SAHTIN.   When you go, take the actor along with you . . . He'll soon be going anyhow . . . he has learned that exactly half a mile from the end of the earth there is a hospital for orgisms . . .

ACTOR (*sticks his head out over the edge of the stove*). For organisms, blockhead.

SAHTIN.   For organs which are poisoned with alcohol.

ACTOR.   Yes, he will soon be going, very soon! You will see!

BARON.   Who is this 'he,' sire?

ACTOR.   It is I.

BARON. Merci, servant of the goddess, who . . . ah, what is she called? The goddess of the drama, of tragedy . . . what is her name?

ACTOR. The muse, blockhead, no goddess, but muse!

SAHTIN. Lachesis . . . Hera . . . Aphrodite . . . Atropos . . . the devil knows the difference between them . . . and our young adorer of the muse shall leave us . . . the old man has wound him up . . .

BARON. The old man was a fool . . .

ACTOR. And you are ignorant savages. You don't even know who Melpomene is. Heartless . . . you will see— he will leave you! 'Interrupt not your orgy, black souls,' as Beranger says . . . He will soon find the place where there is nothing more . . . absolutely . . .

BARON. Where there is nothing more, sire?

ACTOR. Yes! Nothing more, 'this hole here . . . it shall be my grave . . . I die, faded and powerless.' And you, why do you live? Why?

BARON. Just listen, you—Kean, or Genius and Passion. Don't bellow so.

ACTOR. Hold your snout . . . So I will, I'll roar!

NASTIAH (*raises her head from the table, and waves her arms about*). Roar forever! They may hear it.

BARON. What is the meaning of that, lady?

SAHTIN. Let her chatter, Baron . . . the devil take them both . . . may they scream . . . may they run their heads together . . . go on . . . it has a meaning . . . Don't injure others, as the old man said . . . the pilgrim has made us all rebellious.

KLESHTSCH. He enticed us to start out . . . and knew not himself the way.

BARON. The old man was a charlatan.

NASTIAH.   It is not true! You are yourself a charlatan.

BARON.   Don't chatter, lady.

KLESHTSCH.   He was no friend of truth, the old man
. . . He stood with all his might over against the truth
. . . and in the last thought, he is right . . . of what use
to me all truth, when I haven't a mouthful? There, look
at the prince (*looks towards the* TARTAR) . . . he had
crushed his hand at work . . . now they say, it must come
off . . . there you have the truth.

SAHTIN (*strikes the table with his fist*).   Be still!
Asses! Say nothing ill of the old man. (*More quietly.*)
You, Baron, are the biggest fool of all . . . you have no
glimmering of sense—and keep on chattering. The old man
a charlatan? What is truth? Mankind is the truth! He had
seized that . . . but you have not! You are as stupid as a
brick in the pavement. I understood him very well, the
old man . . . He did tell them lies, but he lied out of
sympathy, as the devil knows. There are many such
people who lie for brotherly sympathy's sake . . . I know
I have read about it. They lie so beautifully, with such
spirit, so wonderfully. We have such soothing, such con-
ciliating lies . . . And there are lies which justify taking
the anvil away, and the mashed hand of the toiler . . .
which brings charges against the starving . . . I . . .
know these lies . . . He who has a timid heart . . . or
lives at another's table, should be lied to . . . it gives
him courage . . . puts a mantle on his shoulders . . . but
he who is his own master, who is independent, and lives
not from the sweat of another's brow . . . what are lies
to him? The lie is the religion of servant and master . . .
the truth is the inheritance of free men!

BARON. Bravo! Gloriously said! Exactly my idea! You speak . . . like a man of respectability!

SAHTIN. Why shouldn't a scoundrel speak like a respectable man, when the respectable people talk so much like scoundrels? . . . I have forgotten much, but one thing I still keep. The old man? He had a shrewd head on his shoulders . . . He worked on me like acid on an old, dirty coin. To his health, let him live! Pour one . . . (NASTIAH *pours a glass of beer and hands it to* SAHTIN. *He laughs.*) The old man—he lived from within . . . He saw everything with his own eyes . . . I asked him once: 'Grandfather, why do men really live?' . . . (*He tries in voice and manner to imitate* LUKA.) 'Man lives ever to give birth to strength. There live, for example, the carpenters, noisy, miserable people . . . and suddenly in their midst is a carpenter born . . . such a carpenter as the world has never seen: he is above all, no other carpenter can be compared to him. He gives a new face to the whole trade . . . his own face, so to speak . . . and with that simple impulse it has advanced twenty years . . . and so the others live . . . the locksmiths and the shoemakers, and all the rest of the working people . . . and the contractors . . . and the same is true of other classes—all to give birth to strength. Every one thinks that he himself takes up room in the world, but it turns out that he is here for another's benefit—for some one better . . . a hundred years . . . or perhaps longer . . . if we live so long . . . for the sake of genius. (NASTIAH *stares into* SAHTIN'*s face.* KLESHTSCH *stops working on the accordion and does nothing. The* BARON *lets his head sink and drums with his fingers on the table. The* ACTOR *sticks his head over the edge of the stove, and carefully crawls down.* SAHTIN *goes on.*) All, my children, all, live only to give birth to strength. For that reason we must respect everybody. We cannot know who he is, for what purpose born, or what he may fulfill . . . perhaps he has been born for our good fortune . . . or great benefit . . . and especially must we respect the children . . . the little children . . . they must not suffer restraint . . . let them live their lives . . . let them be respected. (*Laughs quietly to himself. Pause.*)

BARON (*thoughtfully*). For the genius . . . Hm, yes . . . that brings to mind my own family . . . an old family . . . back to Catherine's time . . . of the nobility . . . knights . . . we came from France . . . and entered the Russian service . . . dignities accumulated on us . . . Under Nicholas I., my grandfather, Gustav Deville . . . held a high post . . . he was rich . . . Had hundreds of serfs . . . horses . . . a cook . . .

NASTIAH. Don't be lying . . . it's all a swindle . . .

BARON (*springing up*). Wh-at? Nyah . . . say more!

NASTIAH. It's all a fabrication.

BARON (*cries*). A house in Moscow, a house in Petersburg! Coaches . . . escutcheons on the coach door. (KLESHTSCH *takes the accordion and goes to the side R., where he observes the scene.*)

NASTIAH. Never was such a thing.

BARON. Stop chattering! Dozens of footmen . . . I tell you!

NASTIAH (*tantalizing*). None.

BARON. I'll kill you.

NASTIAH. There were no coaches.

SAHTIN. Let up, Nastenka. Don't make him so furious.

BARON. Wait . . . you wench . . . my grandfather—

NASTIAH. You had no grandfather . . . none. (SAHTIN *laughs.*)

BARON (*sinks back on the seat quite out of breath with anger*). Sahtin, I tell you . . . the harlot . . . what— you laugh, too? And you . . . Won't believe me? (*Cries out desperately, striking the table with his fists.*) Go to the devil . . . all was as I say.

NASTIAH (*in a triumphant tone*). Ah, ha! See how you bellow out! Now you know how a person feels when nobody believes him.

KLESHTSCH (*returns to table*). I thought we should have a fight.

TARTAR. Stupid people . . . childish.

BARON. I . . . I'll not be made a fool of . . . I have proof . . . I have documents to satisfy . . .

SAHTIN. Throw them in the stove . . . And forget your grandfather's coach. In the coach of the past nobody gets anywhere.

BARON. How can she dare . . .

NASTIAH. Hear the noise he is making . . . oh, Lord, how dare I?

SAHTIN. But you see, she dares it. Is she still worse then you? Since she has certainly had in her past no coach and no grandfather . . . perhaps not even a father and mother . . .

BARON (*quieting himself*). Go to the devil . . . You reason everything out so coldbloodedly, while I . . . I believe I have no temper . . .

SAHTIN. Make yourself one. It is a useful thing . . . (*Pause*). Tell me, Nastiah, do you not go often to the hospital?

NASTIAH. What for?

SAHTIN.   To Nastasha?

NASTIAH.   Why, have you dropped from Heaven? She has long been out . . . out and gone . . . Nowhere is she to be found . . .

SAHTIN.   Gone? Disappeared?

KLESHTSCH.   I would like to know whether Waska got Wassilissa into trouble or Wassilissa, Waska.

NASTIAH.   Wassilissa? She will lie herself out. She is crafty. She will send Waska to the mines . . .

SAHTIN.   For manslaughter in a row, only imprisonment . . .

NASTIAH.   Shame. Hard labor would be better. You ought to be sentenced to hard labor, too. You ought to be swept away like a pile of trash . . . into a ditch.

SAHTIN (*taken aback*).   What are you talking about. You are certainly mad.

BARON.   I'll box your ears . . . impertinent hussy.

NASTIAH.   Try it once, just touch me!

BARON.   Certainly I'll try it!

SAHTIN.   Let her be. Don't touch her. Don't insult any one. I always remember the old man. (*Laughs aloud.*) Don't insult mankind, not in her . . . And if I should be insulted so that my reputation was forever gone . . . What should I then do . . . Forgive. No and never!

BARON (*to* NASTIAH).   Mark you! you: I am not one of your kind . . . you . . . wench . . .

NASTIAH.   Ah, you wretch! You . . . you live with me like a maggot in an apple. (*The men laugh understandingly*).

KLESHTSCH.   Silly goose! A fine apple you are . . .

BARON.   Shall a man get mad . . . over such . . . an idiot?

NASTIAH.   You laugh? Don't sham! You don't feel like laughing . . .

ACTOR (*darkly*).   Give him what is his.

NASTIAH.   If I only . . . could: I would take you all and . . . (*Takes a cup from the table and smashes it on the floor*)   like that!

TARTAR.   What are you breaking the dishes for . . . dunce?

BARON (*rising*).   No, I must teach her manners.

NASTIAH (*going out*).   Go to the devil.

SAHTIN (*calls after her*).   Let up, will you? Why do you treat her so? Will you frighten her?

NASTIAH.   You wolves! It is time you were dead. (*Ex. L. U. E.*).

ACTOR (*darkly*).   Amen!

TARTAR.   Ugh, mad folks these Russian women! Hussies, unmanageable. The Tartar women are not so, they know the law.

KLESHTSCH.   She must be given something that she will remember.

BARON.   A low-born creature.

KLESHTSCH (*tries the accordion*).   Ready, and your owner is not to be seen . . . The boy is a lively one.

SAHTIN.   Now have a drink!

KLESHTSCH (*drinks*).   Thanks! It is time to be turning in . . .

SAHTIN.   You'll fall in with our habits after awhile, eh?

KLESHTSCH (*drinks and goes to the pritsche in the corner*).   If I do . . . Everywhere, finally, people are to be found . . . You do not see them at first . . . but later, when you see truer, people are to be found everywhere . . . and they are not so bad after all . . . (*The

TARTAR *spreads a cloth out over the pritsche, sits down and prays.*)

BARON (*to* SAHTIN, *pointing to the* TARTAR). Look though.

SAHTIN. Let him alone . . . He is a good fellow . . . Don't disturb him! (*Laughs aloud*). I am so chicken hearted today . . . The devil may know what's coming.

BARON. You are always a little chicken hearted when you have some spirits in you, . . . and rational then.

SAHTIN. When I am drunk everything pleases me. Hm—yes . . . He prays? Very beautiful of him. A man can believe or not believe . . . that rests with him. Man is free . . . he is responsible to himself for everything: for his belief, his unbelief, his love, his wisdom. Man himself bears the cost of all, is therefore—free . . . Man—that is the truth! But what's man? Not you, nor I, nor they— no, but you, I, old Luka, Napoleon, Mohammed . . . all in one . . . is man. (*Draws in the air the outline of a man's form.*) Comprehend! It is—something huge, in- cluding all beginnings and all endings . . . all is man, all is for man. Only man alone exists—the rest is the work of his hand and his brow. M-an! phenomenal. How loftily it sounds, M-a-n! We must respect man . . . not com- passion . . . degrade him not with pity . . . but respect. Drink we, to the health of man, baron. How splendid it is to feel yourself a man. I . . . I, a former convict, a manslaughter, a cheat . . . yes, when I pass along the street, the people stare at me, as though I were the most desperate of thieves . . . they get out of my way, they look after me . . . and often say to me, thief, why don't you work? . . . Work? What for? To become satiated. (*Laughs aloud.*) I have always hated those who eat themselves to death. It comes to nothing, baron, to nothing. The man is the principal thing, man stands higher than a full stomach. (*Rises from his place.*)

BARON (*shakes his head*). You are a contemplator . . . that is wise . . . that warms my heart . . . I can't do it. (*Looks around carefully and continues in a lower tone.*) I am sometimes afraid, brother . . . do you understand. I fear what may come next.

SAHTIN (*goes up and down*). Nonsense, what shall man fear?

BARON. As far back as I can remember, it always seemed to me as though a fog lay on my brow. I never knew very well just what was the matter, was never at ease . . . I felt as if my whole life long I had only put on my clothes and taken them off again . . . why? No idea! I studied . . . I wore the uniform of an institute for the nobility . . . but what I have learned, I don't know . . . I married . . . put on a frock coat, then a night gown . . . selected a detestable wife—why? I don't understand . . . I went through everything—and wore a shabby gray jacket and red fuzzy trousers . . . but I finally went to the dogs. Hardly took any notice of it. I was employed at the Kameral Court . . . had a uniform, a cap with cockade . . . I embezzled government money . . . pulled on the convict's jacket . . . then—what I have on now . . . and all . . . as if in a dream . . . funny, eh?

SAHTIN. Not very . . . I find it rather foolish.

BARON. Yes . . . I think it was foolish . . . But I must have been born for something . . . eh?

SAHTIN (*laughs*). It is possible . . . Man is born to give birth again to strength. (*Nods his head*). So . . . fine idea.

BARON.   This . . . Natasjka . . . Simply ran out . . .
I will see where she has hidden . . . Still, she . . . (*Ex.
L. U. E. Pause.*)

ACTOR.   You Tartar! (*Pause.*)   Prince! (*The* TARTAR
*turns his head.*)   Pray for me.

TARTAR.   What do you want?

ACTOR (*softly*).   You must pray . . . for me . . .

TARTAR (*after a short silence*).   Pray for yourself.

ACTOR (*climbs quickly down from the stove, mounts the
table, pours a glass of whisky with trembling hand, drinks
and goes out hastily, almost running, L. U. E.*)   Now, I
go!

SAHTIN.   Heh, you, Sigambrer!  Where to? (*He
whistles.* MEDVIÉDEFF *in a wadded woman's jacket, and*
BUBNOFF, *enter R. U. E.* BUBNOFF *carries in one hand a
bundle of pretzels, in the other a couple of smoked fish,
under his arm a bottle of whisky, and in his coat pocket a
second.*)

MEDVIÉDEFF.   The camel is . . . a sort of ass, so to
speak. Only it has no ears.

BUBNOFF.   Let up! You yourself . . . are a sort of
jackass.

MEDVIÉDEFF.   The camel has no ears at all. It hears with
the noseholes.

BUBNOFF (*to* SAHTIN).   Friend of my heart, I have
searched for you in every barroom and dive. Take the
bottle out, my hands are full.

SAHTIN.   Put the pretzels on the table and then you
will have a free hand.

BUBNOFF.   That's right . . . you know the law . . .
you have a sly head . . .

MEDVIÉDEFF. All scoundrels have sly heads . . . I know that . . . long. How could they catch anything without slyness. A law-abiding citizen can be stupid, but a thief must have brains in his head. But about this camel, brother, you are wrong there . . . a camel is a sort of riding deer, I say . . . it has no horns . . . and also no teeth . . .

BUBNOFF. Where hides the whole society. No men here. Say you, come out . . . I treat today . . . who sits there in the corner?

SAHTIN. You have already spent almost everything, scarecrow.

BUBNOFF. Of course, this time my capital was small . . . which I had scraped together . . . Krivoi Zoba! Where is Krivoi Zoba?

KLESHTSCH (*steps to the table*). He is not there.

BUBNOFF. U-u-rrr! Bull dog. Brrju, Brlyu, Brlyu, turkey cock! Don't be barking and snarling! Drink, feast, don't let the head hang . . . I invite all, freely. I love to do that, brother! If I was a rich man, I would have a barroom in which everything would be free, by God, with music and a choir of singers. Come, drink, eat, do you hear, quicken your souls. Come to me, poor men, to my free barroom, Sahtin! Brother! I would you . . . there, take half my entire capital, there, take it.

SAHTIN. Oh, give it all to me . . .

BUBNOFF. All? My whole capital? Would you have? . . . There! A ruble . . . another . . . a twenty . . . a couple of fivers . . . a pair of two copec pieces . . . that is all!

SAHTIN. Lovely . . . I'll keep it safely . . . I'll win my money back with it.

MEDVIÉDEFF. I am a witness . . . you have given him the money in trust . . . how much was it, though?

BUBNOFF. You? You are—a camel . . . We need no witnesses.

ALYOSCHKA (*enters L. U. E. with bare feet*). Children! I have gotten my feet wet!

BUBNOFF. Come—get your gullet wet . . . to balance matters. You're a lovely boy, you sing and make music . . . very clever of you! But—drink . . . not too much! Guzzling is very injurious, brother . . . very injurious . . .

ALYOSCHKA. I see that in you . . . you only look like a man after you have gotten drunk. Kleshtsch! Is my accordion mended? (*Sings and dances with it.*)

> If I were not such a tasty boy,
>     So lively, fresh and neat,
> Then Madam Godfather would
>     Never again call me sweet.

Frozen stiff, children. It is cold.

MEDVIÉDEFF. Hm—and if I may be bold enough to ask: Who is Madam Godfather?

BUBNOFF. You . . . are not interested in that! You have nothing to ask here now. You are no policeman any more . . . that's true. Neither police nor uncle. . . .

ALYOSCHKA. But simply, auntie's husband!

BUBNOFF. Of your nieces, one sits in prison, the other is dying . . .

MEDVIÉDEFF (*expands his chest*). That is not true: She is not dying. She has simply gone away! (SAHTIN *laughs aloud.*)

BUBNOFF.   Quite true, brother! A man without nieces
—is no uncle!

ALYOSCHKA.   Your excellency, cashiered has been,
And Madam Godfather has money,
While I have not even a cent,
But still I'm nice, I'm very nice,
I'm nice and as sweet as new honey.

Brr, it is cold. (KRIVOI ZOBA *enters, then until the end of
the act couples, men and women, enter, undress themselves, stretch out on the pritsches and grumble to themselves.*)

KRIVOI ZOBA.   Why did you run away, Bubnoff?

BUBNOFF.   Come here and sit down. Let's sing something, brother! My favorite hymn, eh?

TARTAR.   It is night now, time for sleeping. Sing during the day.

SAHTIN.   Let them sing, prince, come over here.

TARTAR.   Let them sing—and then a row . . . You
sing and they fight.

BUBNOFF (*going to him*).   What's the matter with your
hand, prince. Has somebody cut it off?

TARTAR.   Why cut it off? Let us wait . . . Perhaps it
will not be necessary to cut it off . . . a hand is not made
of iron . . . that cutting off is quickly done . . .

KRIVOI ZOBA.   It is a bad job, Hassanka! What, are you
without a hand? In our business they only look at the
hands and the back . . . A man without a hand is no man
at all! Might as well be dead. Come, drink a glass with us.

KVASHNYA (*enters L. U. E.*).   Ah, my dear tenants.
Biting cold outside, slush . . . and raw . . . Is my policeman there? Heh, there, Commissioner!

MEDVIÉDEFF.   Here I am.

KVASCHNYA.   You have my jacket on again? What is the matter with you? You have been having a bit, eh? That don't go.

MEDVIÉDEFF.   Bubnoff . . . has a birthday . . . and it is so cold, such slush . . .

KVASCHNYA.   I'll teach you . . . such slush . . . But don't forget the rules of this household . . . go to bed . . .

MEDVIÉDEFF (*Ex. R. to kitchen*).   To bed! I can . . . I will . . . it is time. (*Ex.*)

SAHTIN.   Why then are you . . . so strict with him?

KVASCHNYA.   There is nothing else to do, dear friend. A man like that must be closely reined. I did not marry him for fun. He is military, I thought . . . and you are a dangerous lot . . . I, a woman, would be no match for you . . . now he begins to souse—no, my boy, that don't go.

SAHTIN.   You made a bad selection in your assistant . . .

KVASCHNYA.   No, wait—he is all right . . . you will not get me . . . and if you did the honeymoon would not last over a week . . . you'd gamble the clothes off my back.

SAHTIN (*laughs*).   That's no lie, I would lose you . . .

KVASCHNYA.   So, then. Alyoschka.

ALYOSCHKA.   Here he is . . .

KVASCHNYA.   Tell me, what gossip have you been spreading about me?

ALYOSCHKA.   I? Everything! I tell everything that can honestly be told. That is a woman, say I. Simply an astonishing woman. Flesh, fat, bones, over three hundred weight, and brains, not half a grain.

KVASCHNYA.   Nyah, you lie, my young man, I have

quantities of brain . . . No—why do you tell folks that I beat my policeman?

ALYOSCHKA.   I thought, because you tore his hair out . . . that is as good as beating.

KVASCHNYA (*laughs*).   You are a fool! Why carry such dirt out of the house . . . that has grieved him sorely . . . he has taken to drink from worry over your gossip.

ALYOSCHKA.   Listen: It is therefore true, what the proverb says: that the hen has a throat for liquor. (SAHTIN *and* KLESHTSCH *laugh*.)

KVASCHNYA.   But you are witty: and tell me, what sort of fruit you are, Alyoschka?

ALYOSCHKA.   I am a fellow who fits snugly in the world. The finest of the finest sort! A regular jack of all trades. Where my eye turns, there my heart follows.

BUBNOFF (*on the* TARTAR's *pritsche*).   Come, we will not let you sleep. Today we'll sing . . . the whole night, eh, Krivoi Zoba?

KRIVOI ZOBA.   May we?

ALYOSCHKA.   I'll play for you . . .

SAHTIN.   And we will hear it.

TARTAR (*grunting*).   Nyah, old satan, Bubna . . . pour me a glass: 'We'll revel, we'll drink until death gives the wink.'

BUBNOFF.   Pour him one, Sahtin! Krivoi Zoba, sit down! Ah, brothers! How little a man needs! I, for example, I've only had a couple of swallows . . . and walk tangled footed. Krivoi Zoba, strike up . . . my favorite song. I will sing and weep.

KRIVOI ZOBA (*sings*.)   'Though still the sun goes up and down . . .'

BUBNOFF (*falls in*). 'No gleam can pierce to me in here.' (*The door is jerked open.*)

BARON (*on the platform, crying*). Heh, there . . . you! Come quick . . . (*Silence, all stare at the* BARON. *Behind him appears Nastiah who with staring eyes goes to the table.*)

SAHTIN (*softly*). He must spoil our song . . . the fool.

CURTAIN

## Theater:

COUNTESS JULIE. August Strindberg see THREE PLAYS

DREAMY KID. Eugene O'Neill, see FIVE MODERN PLAYS

FAREWELL SUPPER. Arthur Schnitzler, see FIVE MODERN PLAYS

FATHER (THE). August Strindberg. 1434-9 $3.95

FIVE MODERN PLAYS: *Dreamy Kid, Farewell Supper, Sisters Tragedy, Lost Silk Hat, Intruder*. 1435-7 $5.95

IMPORTANCE OF BEING EARNEST. Oscar Wilde. 1442-x $3.95

INTRUDER. Maurice Maeterlinck, see FIVE MODERN PLAYS.

IRISH PLAYS--THREE. *Land of Heart's Desire, Twisting of the Rope, Riders to the Sea*. 1457-8 $5.95

LAND OF HEART'S DESIRE. W. B. Yeats, see IRISH PLAYS (THREE)

LOST SILK HAT. Edward Dunsany, see FIVE MODERN PLAYS

LOWER DEPTHS. Maxim Gorki. Translated from the Russian by Edwin Hopkins. 1445-4 $4.95

OUTLAW. August Strindberg, see THREE PLAYS

RIDERS TO THE SEA. John M. Synge, see IRISH PLAYS (THREE)

SALOMÉ. Oscar Wilde, Illustrated by Aubrey Beardsley. 1467-5 $3.95

SEA GULL and TRAGEDIAN IN SPITE OF HIMSELF. Anton Chekhov. Trans. by O. F. Murphy. 1454-3 $4.95

SECOND SHEPHERD PLAY. Lisl Beer. 1246-x $3.95

SISTERS TRAGEDY. Richard Hughes, see FIVE MODERN PLAYS

STRONGER. Auguste Strindberg, see THREE PLAYS

THREE PLAYS. *Countess Julie, Stronger, Outlaw*. A. Strindberg. Trans. by and with notes by E. & W. Oland. 1458-6 $5.95

TWISTING OF THE ROPE. Douglas Hyde, see IRISH PLAYS (THREE)

## Essays, Short Stories, Poetry:

ARMOURY LIGHT VERSE. Richard Armour. 1424-1 $3.95

BEOWULF. Translated from Old English by Albert Haley. 1713-5 $7.95

BRAZILIAN TALES. Attendant's Confession, Fortune Teller, Aunt Zeze Tears, Pigeons. 1426-8 $4.95

CANTERVILLE GHOST. Oscar Wilde. 1429-2 $3.95

CARGOES--BEST SEA STORIES. W.W. Jacobs. 1430-6 $4.95

CIVIL DISOBEDIENCE. H. D. Thoreau. Edited by E. Brown. *Modern Essays*. 1449-7 $3.95

COLOURED STARS--FIFTY ASIATIC LOVE SONGS. Edward Mathers. 1432-2 $3.95

FAMOUS STORIES FROM FOREIGN COUNTRIES. 1433-0 $4.95

FULL MOON IS RISING. Basho. Japanese haikus. 1651-1 $15.95 c.

GITANJALI. R. Tagore. Introduction by W. B. Yeats. 1436-5 $3.95

GOLD BUG. Edgar A. Poe. Illustrations by Mittis. 1437-3 $3.95

GREATEST THING IN THE WORLD. Henry Drummond. Introduction by Elizabeth Towne. 1438-1 $3.95

HOUND OF HEAVEN. Francis Thompson. Introduction by G.K. Chesterton. 1440-3 $3.95

INFERNO. Dante. Modern English translation. Illustrated. 1884-0 $9.95

ISSUES IN BILINGUAL EDUCATION. Adolph Caso. 1721-6 $11.95

JIG FORSLING. A symphonic poem by Conrad Aikin. 1433-8 $3.95

LAST LION AND OTHER STORIES. Blasco-Ibanez. Introduction by M. J. Lorente. 1444-6 $3.95

LATIN DICTIONARIES Kunzer (Vergil, Cicero, Caesar) $3.95 each.

MAN WHO WOULD BE KING. Rudyard Kipling. *Two Tales*. Int. by W. Follett. 1460-8 $3.95

MASS MEDIA VS THE ITALIAN AMERICANS. Adolph Caso. How the Italian Americans are depicted in the media. 1831-x $7.95

MAXIMS. LaRouchefaucauld. Translated by John Heard. 1448-9 $3.95

ON CRIMES AND PUNISHMENTS. Cesare Beccaria. Introduction by A. Caso. 1800-x $5.95

PIT AND THE PENDULUM. Edgar A. Poe, see GOLD BUG.

REEDS & MUD. Blasco-Ibanez. 1470-5 $7.95

RUBAIYAT. Omar Khayyam. Translated by Edward Fitzgerald, illustrations by Elihu Vedder. 1452-7 $3.95

SHROPSHIRE LAD. Alfred E. Housman. Introduction by W.S. Braithwaite, illustrations by J. R. Brown. 1455-1 $3.95

SYMPOSIUM OF PLATO. Plato. Int. by Benjamin Jowett. 1456-x $3.95

VILLON--THE BOOK OF. Francois Villon. Translated from Old French by A. C. Swinburne. 1425-x $3.95

WISDOM OF CONFUCIOUS. Confucius. 1462-4 $3.95